DARK PLACE

JEFF VANOUDENHOVE

JAVO
PUBLICATION

Westfield, MA

JAVO Publication
125 Ridgecrest Drive
Westfield, Massachusetts 01085

This is a work of fiction. The characters, places, and events portrayed in this book are either the product of the author's imagination or are used fictitiously. Any similarity to real persons, living or dead, business establishments, or events is coincidental and not intended by the author.

ISBN 978-1-7356173-0-5
Library of Congress Control Number: 2020916404

Cover and Title Page artwork by Joseph Weymouth

For my Mom-
Who sadly passed before this book's completion.
You are forever in my heart.

Acknowledgments

I am not entirely sure I would have been able to finish this novel if it hadn't been for Elizabeth Kelly and her proofreading and editing skills. She helped make this a better story than it would have been without her help. Thank you, Liz. Thank you also goes out to Dave Whiteley for his words of encouragement, whose honesty with his critiques helped bring about the prologue of the story. Thanks to Venessa Clark for being a beta reader of my first draft. I want to thank Joe Weymouth for his incredible cover artwork which shows a persistence to achieve perfection in his designs. I also want to give a quick shout out to Jason Reipold for reminding me several times that I have a book to finish. Finally, thank you to my wife, Elena, for being patient with me while writing this book. It took time away from the two of us, but your understanding helped me through it to the end.

Enter: The Darkness

We are all born with a certain light inside us. We are all born with hope. We are all born innocent. It is a constant struggle however, to maintain that hope; to maintain that light that we so desperately want to hold onto. When does the darkness begin to set in? How can one prevent it from consuming their very soul? It latches onto us with a vice-like grip and does not want to let go. Eventually, our lives are inexplicably changed by the ever-growing darkness that begins to infect us.

Some are affected by the external darkness that continually surrounds them. So many of the people and the places and the things they interact with find subtle ways to negatively impact their delicate psyches. They, in turn, negatively affect others.

James dealt with that in his life. I only wish I had seen it sooner. Brothers are supposed to take care of one another. But how was I to stop him from doing what he did? And what happened to him didn't just affect his life, but it also negatively impacted me. And not just me, but our mom as well.

There were others too. The Gradies seemed nice enough; for awhile. The pressures of their new job opportunities and the new community they found themselves in quickly began to change them. And it wasn't for the better. That, and their actions toward others within the community, began to affect the demeanor of those around them.

Then, there are some that must live with a deeper internal struggle to keep the darkness that lingers within from growing and tearing them apart.

Troy comes to mind. He was my brother's childhood nemesis. He turned out all right in the end after he lost almost everything in his life. But he didn't start that way. He had hatred brewing inside of him from early on and for such a long time. He struggled with the dark most of his life. And nobody knew why. Some people are just like that, I guess.

The local grocery store owner, Mr. Sloan, also had to fight to keep his dark impulses in check. That man would have ended up in prison had he acted on any of them. He didn't have a hatred for others like Troy did. On the contrary. His darkness was purely lustful by nature. Had he not found the strength to keep his urges from surfacing, there's no telling how many young, innocent girls he may have infected with his sickness. How many lives would have been torn apart before a brave one finally stepped forward to tell her story?

Even our mom let the darkness take hold of her. She wrestled with it for a time but it was too strong. Once the seed was planted, it grew ever so stronger every day. I'd like to think it all started with the incident involving my brother James, but when I look back I can see the darkness was already burning her up inside trying to get out. After James... well, I think she just gave up trying to fight it anymore.

Then there's me. I am one of the unlucky few to be afflicted with both the internal darkness that will continue to feed upon me until its hunger is quenched and the external darkness that is festering around me like some God-forsaken plague. It's all I can do to open my eyes each morning. It has become a challenge to fight off the fatigue, the hunger, the loneliness that overtakes me each day.

I try to occupy my thoughts with the better times in my life, but the darkness encompassing me is so overwhelming that even the better times I now realize were mingled with instances of the dark lurking about, waiting to consume my very essence.

Will it ever end? Can I find my way back from this ever-darkening place that has taken control of my being? Is it too much to hope for? We are all born with hope after all. We are all born with a certain light inside us. But the dark quickly extinguishes the light. What is it they say? "Every dark cloud has a silver lining." "There's a light at the end of the tunnel." "It's always darkest right before the dawn." That implies a certain level of confidence that the dawn will surely come. Maybe it will. Am I ready to believe that? I want to. Yes, I know it will come, but for now, one thing is certain…

…The dark is upon us.

Chapter 1

All Consuming

It has been some time since I have seen the light; the bright, warm feeling of openness surrounding me. Clean, clear air for as far as the eyes could see. The sun… oh the beautiful, soothing rays of the sun… what I wouldn't give to feel its warmth beating down on me from above. The beautiful, wonderful smell of trees and freshly cut grass overwhelming my senses as the wind would take hold of it. As I recall, there were other savory scents from my younger days that my memory suddenly dredges up. They remind me that life hasn't always been as damp and dreary as this eternal darkness that seems to engulf my very being. I question why I punish myself of late with these scrambled thoughts that pierce my soul as much as my brain. Then a calm clarity sweeps across my fragmented psyche to let me know that it is such memories as these that help to keep my sanity in check. Such memories as...

Every Sunday morning you could bet that the aroma of a newly-baked, hot apple pie would be emanating from Mrs. Kaplan's kitchen window next door. Some weeks she would bake a rhubarb pie, or a nice, fat, peach cobbler; but most of the time it was apple. She had a small orchard growing in the field adjacent to her house. All the kids from around the block would help her pick the apples; mostly because they wanted to take some home with them. She didn't mind. She was getting old and didn't have anybody to help her around the house, so any number of apples the kids could gather up for her was a welcome blessing. I always felt somewhat sorry for her. Things just didn't seem exactly right with her after her husband died. I suppose any person wouldn't be right after losing their companion of forty-six years.

Mom used to make me and my brother go over her house after school to see if she had any household chores that needed to be done. She always had something that needed fixing, but most times they were things that a ten and twelve-year-old couldn't handle by themselves. She always kept us busy on the small stuff though. Free pies and candy were our payment each week. Mom didn't like us eating candy, so we would hide it away when we got home so we could enjoy it later just before bed. It may not have been good for our teeth, but it sure was good for our taste buds. Mom did, however, appreciate the pies. She was pretty good at baking pies herself, but nothing compared to the delectable taste of Mrs. Kaplan's pies. And since my brother and I earned a pie just about every week, that freed mom up to do other things around the house. After all, "There isn't enough time in the day" she used to tell us. I guess being a single mother with two kids to take care of can keep a person quite busy. And she *was* too.

Most people in town knew she worked all the time to try and make ends meet. She would work extra hours, late nights, weekends; just about anything she could do to pay the bills and keep food on the table. It wasn't the greatest job in the world, working at Sloan's Market, but it was all my mother thought she was qualified for. She didn't have much of an education. She was incredibly bright and intuitive, very articulate, and had a great sense of dedication, but she never went to college. She dropped out of high school actually, at the age of sixteen. The way the times were, nobody would hire you without a college degree, and they wouldn't even look at you if you didn't have your high school diploma. Luckily for my mom, Mr. Sloan had a little thing for her. I guess you could call it a crush even at his age. He was ten years older than my mother but he liked her something fierce. Not just her actually, but any woman that was within a forty-foot radius of him and somewhat attractive. When mom was twenty years old and inquired about any job openings he might have, Mr. Sloan jumped at the chance to hire her. And there she stayed too, until the day she died.

That thought quickly snaps me back to my present harsh reality. It's cold in here today. It's cold every day, but today feels especially cold. My breath breaks the still, stagnant air every time I exhale. It's something I've become accustomed to. My fingertips have barely a feeling left in them, but they are not so numb that I can't feel the ridges that have taken residence along my palms from the condensation that clings densely on the surrounding walls. Instantly, another memory tugs at me from another time.

It takes me back to those winters when James and I would spend all day outside building snow forts and having snowball fights. We would stay out so long that it felt like our fingers and toes were going to fall off from frostbite. When we would eventually make our way back inside, we knew that mom would be waiting for us with the water already brewed to whip up some delicious hot cocoa to warm us up. The sweet taste of the chocolate was always so inviting; with small marshmallows perfectly melted on top forming a thin layer of white that can only be described as heaven in a cup. Even though it felt so good to get back in from the cold and thaw out a bit, my brother and I could only think about getting back out to the battlefield of our frozen kingdom to see which of us would reign supreme for the day.

Occasionally, mom would let us take our sled to Parkers' Field. It wasn't really "Parkers' Field" anymore, seeing as how the last remaining Parker hadn't lived there in about twenty years or more, but everyone still called it that. We had great times there; making jumps out of any snow mounds we deemed worthy of our trusty sled. What did my brother call her…? It's been so long since I even thought of those days. "Trailblazer!" That's right. She was the fastest sled on Wurlton Street. Heck, maybe even the fastest in the whole town. Every kid on the block would relish in the chance to even get a glimpse of Ol' Trailblazer. They all wanted her for their own. She was an old-time, wooden-top sled with two iron ski rails underneath, a brake in the back, and a whole lot of speed all over. It was strange how it showed up on our doorstep one day with a note on it that read "Enjoy." Mom said it was from our dad; although we didn't understand why he would have sent us a sled out of the blue. What reasoning could he have had to do such a thing? We didn't know him after all. Not really. And he didn't know us. Still, it was a welcome surprise, and an even better, fun-filled couple of winters. It would have been longer too, if not for that rotten, troublemaking Troy Thompson.

That boy had hate following him wherever he went. He was always looking for trouble, and when he couldn't find it, he'd start it. He was a crass, hotheaded young boy with no manners to speak of. He was all mouth, and he had the body to back up his words. All the kids in the neighborhood tried their best to stay clear of him. All the kids, except my brother that is. James was the only other kid on the block who had a little bulk to him. He wasn't quite as big as Troy Thompson, but you still didn't want to upset him too much for fear that he would put a hurtin' on you something fierce.

I still remember that day when Troy took Trailblazer right from James' hands. The scuffle that followed was one I'll never forget. I had never seen my brother so heated before. His blood was boiling for sure and his eyes were swallowed with pure rage. James threw the first punch, but it glanced off Troy's shoulder as he twisted to avoid the blow. Before my brother had a chance to throw a second punch, Troy belted James in the mouth knocking him to the ground. I remember seeing trickles of blood on the snow where he landed, but he rose right back up to defend himself. The two of them exchanged fisticuffs for what seemed like hours. In truth, it was only for about three minutes. Troy was just too big and strong for my brother to withstand any longer than that. When it was over, my brother was lying bloodied on the hardened white snow. A devilish smirk ran across the victor's face as he walked off with Trailblazer; our trusty winter companion. I helped my brother back to his feet and we slowly made our way through the crowd of children's faces that had gathered to watch the one-sided brawl. Everyone remained silent as we walked away with our heads down. We couldn't stand the thought of looking anyone in the eyes. When we got home, we went to our room and cried for the rest of the night. She was gone. Troy took Trailblazer that day and we never saw her again. We couldn't even hold onto the only thing our father ever gave us.

Once again, woeful snapshots from a time long past kicks me back to the here and now. The concrete floor and walls are very hard, but I've grown accustomed to it. It's very wet and dank today. Much like my hands, my bare feet are also quite wrinkled from time spent pressed against the damp surface beneath me. There is little room to move, and even less reason to want to try. Hopelessness engulfed me... I don't know... years ago. Has it been years? Perhaps it's been decades? It makes no sense to try to keep track anymore. Time has no meaning here.

Funny, I remember those words; "Time has no meaning". Mr. Frank, my psychology professor, once stated that "time is nothing and everything all at once, therefore time has no meaning". I can't understand why that has stuck with me all this time. It didn't even make sense to me back then. I'm not sure it makes sense to me now. But for some reason, those words have remained burned into my memory. As if my knowledge of time was somehow supposed to help me. It didn't help me when I got kicked out of college. And it didn't help me even after when I got laid off from the plant? It would have been nice knowing how time was going to help me back then because it sure doesn't help me now. No, it's the memories that keep me going now; the memories of the good times in my life; the simpler times.

I remember when I hit an inside-the-park home run during the annual "Summer Day Festival" ballgame. It was the first time I had ever done such a thing, and also the first and only time that the annual game had ever been won in such a fashion. It was so exciting, and mom was so proud of me.

I remember when little Tommy Dugan spent his entire allowance on candy from Sloan's Market. He just about cleared out the entire aisle that day. Of course, he had so much candy that he had to share it with a bunch of us kids. It was the only way to get rid of the evidence before his folks found out what he had done.

I also remember my Prom. That's a night I'll never forget. The way that Jasmine looked that night was just about enough to make a man's heart stop ticking right there on the dance floor.

When she was younger, Jasmine had always been a small, frail-looking thing. She had legs that were as thin as Popsicle sticks; her thick, red hair was always scraggly. She had freckles covering most of her face and arms. She wasn't too much to look at really. Her folks had moved to town when she was ten, so she earned the title "outsider" before she even stepped out of the car.

They bought the Miller's old residence that had been abandoned for about four years after Mrs. Miller just packed up and moved away. She left everything behind after her husband had gotten himself killed in a freak tractor accident. After a year or so, the bank took possession of the property and tried to sell it several times, but with no luck. It seemed nobody had the heart to buy the house knowing what had happened, and the circumstances behind why it was left abandoned. Well, nobody local anyway. But the Gradies weren't local, and they didn't know the story. Either that or they didn't care. They were just looking for an affordable house to start their fresh new life in. I heard that they had gotten a really good deal on it too. It was practically a steal.

Mr. Gradie got himself a job as the vice president of our town's bank and moved his family here from Arkansas. It wasn't long before he started turning people who were looking for loans away for one reason or another.

Mrs. Gradie took up teaching as a substitute teacher until she finally managed to catch a break at the middle school and was hired as a fulltime sixth-grade teacher. Thankfully I was already in the eighth grade by then. I never had to endure her misdirected, politically-filled bantering in the classroom as she "pretended" to impart her knowledge into the "leaders of tomorrow," as she would call her students.

The Gradies weren't any different than the rest of the folks in town, but they sure acted like they were better. Because of it, their daughter Jasmine received an unfair share of inflammatory injustices and negative criticisms from most of the kids around town.

Jasmine was five months younger than me, so I too was one who fell into that category of harassing kids. We all knew she didn't deserve it. She just got stuck paying for her parent's transgressions. But it's the way life is I guess. It wasn't for too much longer though, that she had to endure the unflattering remarks and childlike behavior. As soon as that girl started growing into her looks, she had the boys in her class fawning all over her. She would feed into it too. She would give someone a wink or a long seductive glance; soon she had that person eating right out of her hands.

"Stay away from that one, little brother," James would warn me. "Nothing good can come of it."

And I listened too, for a couple of years anyway. I would purposely find reasons to avoid her. I wouldn't allow her hypnotic stare to pierce through my protective barrier and trap me in her hex, like she had done to so many others, only to discard them like yesterday's newspaper. It all seemed to work out nicely too... until Prom.

The morning of the Prom was no different than any other morning that had come in the past four years of high school, except that this day was going to have classes filled with students that were even less interested in the day's academic curriculum than usual. The buzz all around school that morning was about who was going to the Prom with whom; who wasn't going, and why weren't they going? The teachers seemed just about as unenthusiastic about teaching as the students did about learning. It's just as well, I remember thinking. After all, I wasn't going to the prom, so why should I be one of the few people that had to pay attention in class when so many others didn't care to?

It was right around the third period when news of the break-up started to spread like wildfire. Jasmine's newest beau didn't wait around to become her latest victim. He decided to take matters into his own hands, and he dumped her that morning. It was only a matter of time before somebody did it to her before she could do it to them. Still, to do it on the morning of the prom was pretty harsh.

There was a strange feeling that crept up inside me. I felt sorry for Jasmine, although to this day I don't understand why. Maybe it wasn't so much that I felt sorry for her. Maybe it was because, if for nothing else, it opened up an opportunity for me to come up with an excuse to be able to make it to the prom. I *did* want to go. After all, it was my Senior Prom. I was just too shy to ask anyone in advance, and there certainly weren't any girls lining up to ask me either. Time just got the better of me; before I knew it, the date had arrived and I was left with nobody to go with. But now, as chance would have it, Jasmine had no one to go with either. I bravely, yet half-heartedly, approached Jasmine in the hallway just after fifth period. It's not what you would consider the most tactful of choices, swooping in so quickly after a failed relationship, but Jasmine's face showed no sign of regret or sorrow from the morning's unfortunate event. Yet for me, it was quite fortunate. As much as I was gathering up the courage to ask her the all-important question, I knew well in advance what the answer was most likely going to be. So, with a slight tremor in my voice, I asked, "Would you like to accompany me to the Prom tonight?" The answer I was expecting never came. Instead, she simply said, "I'd like that," and smiled. I didn't quite know how to react, so I quickly nodded, said "ok," and then as I turned to walk away, dribbled off some quirky response about picking her up later.

And just like that, the memory goes dim, and my reality becomes dark. As cold as it is in this place, the sweat still manages to find its way to the surface of the skin and trickle down my face until it either reaches my mouth, where I lick the salty drop off my lips, or it drips off my chin to the cold, hard floor below. Why am I still here, and when can I go home? I struggle with my feelings and try to recall my last thought. What was it again? Oh yes, the Prom.

I didn't have a tuxedo, so I dressed in one of my brother's nicely pressed suits. He had several nice suits that he had purchased a couple of years back when he started working as a teller at the bank for Mr. Gradie. He hated having to dress up, but it was either that or to work in the meat department at Sloan's Market. He swore he would never work for Mr. Sloan, just to be stuck following the same footsteps that mom had already laid the foundation for. She wanted better of us anyhow. So when the opportunity arose for him to become a bank teller, he took the chance. Now, on prom night, I had become the beneficiary of that decision and the good fortune that James had pretty good taste when it came to suits. He did chide me about taking this particular girl though.

"Didn't I warn you about this one?" he stated with a slight curl in his upper lip.

Defensively, I snapped back, "It doesn't mean anything. We're just going as friends."

"All right, just don't do anything stupid," James said. "She's my boss's daughter."

I had no intention of doing anything stupid, except for maybe when I called her and told her that we should just meet at the prom instead of me picking her up. I didn't want others seeing us arrive together and thinking we were a couple.

I arrived ten minutes late, which I did on purpose because of what my mother used to say. "Always get to where you're going early unless it's something

special. For those times be 'fashionably' late." I'm
not sure I ever learned the reason why, but I always
stuck to that rule. It seemed fitting for this night anyway, and appropriate as well since, by the time I had
arrived, there were only a few pockets of people here
and there. There was very little activity on the dance
floor. Truthfully I didn't know what to expect. I had
never gone to a dance before, and never anywhere
with a girl.

Before I could make my way over to the bever-
age table to get something to drink, something caught
my eye. It was a glimmer from the overhead light that
had reflected off of the tiara that she was wearing.
Jasmine had arrived. I can picture it as if it were yesterday. She wore a long, form-fitting, blue satiny
dress with sequins scattered around the neck and
shoulders. She had white gloves that ran up her fore-
arms to her elbows. Sparkling diamond earrings ac-
cented her freckled face beautifully as they dangled
down from her ears. And of course, the gem covered
tiara that had initially caught my eye displayed magnificently atop her perfectly styled, wavy red hair.
She was outstanding; a stunning sight to see, which
was apparent in the gaping jaws of the awed onlook-
ers as she made her way across the floor to my side. I
remember taking her hand and...

My memory is suddenly halted as something snaps me back to the present. What was that? Did I just hear something? I listen more intently. A creaking noise suddenly disrupts the silence in what has become my sanctuary as much as my hell. Before I can react, I am left with what can only be described as blindness. Is this light? I can't tell. It has been too long since I have seen it, and in truth, I still can't "see" it. My pupils shrink to such a degree that I might as well just shut my eyes. The insides of my eyelids are easier to take. I feel hands grab hold of my arms and legs, and suddenly there is a different kind of feeling that rushes to greet me. One of pain.

Chapter 2

Emergence

As the blood rolls down my back, I can only keep my scattered thoughts long enough before the next wave of lashings takes place. Many times have I felt this stinging sensation, as the metal barbs on the end of the whip gouge into my flesh like so many knives cutting through cooked noodles. Skin rips apart and shreds upon contact of the cold sharp steel. Yes, many times I have felt this, but I can't remember how long it has been since the last time. Why now? What has brought such torment upon me? Again, I hear the cracking sound of the whip just moments before I feel the searing pain of muscle rip-ping from my back. I scream in agony as I drop to my knees. Again and again, the unbearable onslaught of leather and steel pierce into me until the nerve end-ings in my back become so numb that they can no longer carry a pain impulse to my brain. I slowly feel myself slipping away into unconsciousness… and then blackness.

"Edward!"

"Edward Joseph! Come up here. Can you explain this to me?"

It was clear from her tone that mom was not hap-py about something. And the fact that my first name was called out in its full form, followed by my mid-dle name tells me that this may be quite serious. Ra-ther than deal with it, I shrugged it off as I usually did with a snappy retort.

"I'm busy."

It was a comment that had worked many times before and left my mother feeling frustrated enough to drop the subject and walk away. But this time she insisted.

"I don't care how busy you are," she protested, "I want you up here right now."

I breathe out a resenting sigh and manage a slight grumble as I pull the bed covers from my waist and gradually make my way to my feet. The barely lit staircase ahead of me appears to sway back and forth for the briefest of moments as I struggle to gather my balance. My legs feel a little wobbly beneath me as they begin to awaken with the morning's first rise.

As I make my way to the top of the basement stairs, I see my mother sitting at the kitchen table with her head propped up with her left hand and a cigarette clenched tightly between the first two fingers of her right hand. Seeing my mother smoking was always a bad sign. She was not what you would consider a smoker by any means; barely finishing a pack a month. But in times of anxiety or anger, she had been known to light up a stick or two to calm her nerves a bit.

Something that catches my attention even more than the cigarette however, is the piece of paper on the table in front of her that seems to have garnered her full attention. Gazing down at the paper in front of her has allowed her hair, which is normally kept up and neatly pulled back behind her ears, to fall unpleasantly about her face. I move in closer to catch a glimpse of the paper in the hopes that it might be something other than what I already know it must be.

"What is this?" she asks, refusing to even look up at me.

"It's nothing mom, don't worry about it."

I extend my arm to grab the paper from the table, but with no luck. My mother quickly snatches it up and pushes herself backward in an attempt to make it to her feet. It would have been a little more intimidating if she had *actually* made it to her feet in that first attempt. Instead, she faltered and stumbled back onto the chair, only managing to catch enough of the edge to keep her from falling to the floor. Either way, her intention was all too clear just the same. She then composed herself, took a deep breath, and stood up in what could have been described as a threatening manner. Only "could have been," because my mother stood at just five feet four inches tall and only weighed about a hundred and five pounds soaking wet. She wasn't much of a threat to anybody. But she did just brazenly confront me quite angrily as she waved the paper beneath my chin.

"Don't you dare tell me not to worry about it! What did you do this time?"

I stumble for the words that I know will inevitably break her heart. "I… I enlisted."

Mom's face told the story in an instant. My heart dropped into my stomach and a chill ran down my spine causing my fingers to go numb.

"Not you too!" she cried. "Not like your brother. Don't do it. I need you here."

I collected my thoughts, took a deep breath, and began to explain to her how this is something I had to do. It was something that James would have wanted me to do. And I couldn't help but wonder if she too would have wanted this for me, or at least have been proud of my decision if it hadn't been for James not coming back... back... to...

...Back to consciousness. I feel... wet. There has been much blood that has pooled beneath me. How long have I been out? Too long. Or maybe not long enough. Lying on my stomach, I feel an aching pain coming from my back which oddly comes as a comfort to me. It lets me know there isn't any permanent nerve damage. As I struggle to open my eyelids, I feel my right cheek pressed against this cold, hard surface that appears to be a surgical table of some kind. My arms won't budge from my sides; held down firmly with leather straps. I try to scan the room to get a sense of where I am. I haven't been here before. Although it reminds me of the hospital room I was in the day I broke my hand on James' helmet. My mind wanders back.

It was his first time home on leave before shipping off to the Gulf. Jasmine was over the house. She and I had been a couple now for almost a year, and I was acting stupid and showing off to her. My brother was getting so much attention that weekend that I was practically unnoticed by people around town. I didn't want Jasmine thinking I was any less of a man just because I wasn't going off to war like he was. I grabbed my brother's helmet and began bragging how I could put a pretty good dent in it by punching it. I can't even tell you how I came up with the idea. It just popped into my head when I saw it laying there on top of his duffel bag. I asked Jasmine to hold it for me, but she refused, citing that I was going to hurt my hand. So I placed the helmet on the floor, chambered back, and released a blow harder than I thought I had in me. The break was immediate and excruciating. I grabbed my right hand and could feel the bones floating loosely inside my skin. The only thing I accomplished was three broken metacarpals and a sprained wrist. I remember looking down at the helmet to see what damage I had inflicted upon my target in the hopes of at least having salvaged a bit of dignity from that painful mishap. Wouldn't you know it; not a scratch or dent on it. Add to the pain of my now broken hand; a bruised ego.

But that was a long time ago, and the hand has long since healed, as I find myself once again in a similar place to that hospital room, but under completely different circumstances. For what purpose was I brought here? And why was I beaten, to begin with? I had been locked away in that... that place for so long, with nothing but leftover scraps to feed upon and pooled rainwater to drink. I was beginning to think they forgot I was even a person locked away in there instead of some pet.

This room, although larger, cleaner, and brighter than my previous surroundings, still fills me with a sense of dread. The room itself is only about ten feet square. I scan to my left and notice a countertop that spans the length of the room. On it appears to be instruments of some sort, most likely used for surgical applications. From my perspective, it is hard to tell. I tilt my head slightly up to glean what I can of the adjoining wall that is in front of me. A large silver door with a small barred window is positioned in the center with two rolling carts on either side. I can see a bit of the white tiled floor below that has been splattered with blood droplets in a streamlined fashion, starting at the door and continuing to where they disappear from my sight beneath the table I lie on. It is my blood for sure, and perhaps some of it from others as well. I assume there were others, although I can't recall hearing anyone else. I know I haven't seen anyone else, but I can't be the only one, can I? Is this a room for torture, or a room for healing? Does it matter? I am bound here against my will, unable to move, and at the mercy of anyone who enters and decides it is their turn to have their way with me.

As if on cue, the door opens and I quickly close my eyes to feign unconsciousness. I try my best to steady my breathing. I hear the footsteps of two men enter the room and come to a stop at the head of my table. I can feel their eyes staring down at me. A faint smell of aftershave mixed with a hint of... death... hits my senses. Then a smell of cigarettes washes over me. I listen...

"And you believe this one will work?"

"I do. He is recovering quite nicely."

The first man's voice is very guttural with a noticeable wheezing sound. It's quite obvious this is the smoker from which I detected the cigarette smell. The second man's voice is much softer, smoother. He sounds younger.

"When will he be ready?"

"Well, it is hard to say. As you can see, he came to me in quite a bit of a mess. We can fix him up physically, although there is no way of knowing how he will recover psychologically. Your men…"

"Don't question my men doctor. I give the orders, they follow them. That is all that need concern you. You just make sure you do your part. We will handle his… mental stability. Are we clear on that?"

"Of course, sir. I will handle things on my end."

"See that you do. No mistakes this time."

I hear one of the men walk toward the door and out while the other stays behind. The door shuts behind the departed man as I hear the clicking sound of a lock. Momentarily, the room is silent except for a quiet buzzing coming from the florescent lights overhead. Then the silence is broken…

"You can open your eyes, Edward. I know that you're awake."

Surprised, I open my eyes, still unable to see my captor from my vantage point as he stands behind me to my right.

"I've been watching you. You're being watched. Well, you were, but I am here with you now. You can't see it, but there is a camera on the wall behind you."

The man with the soft voice makes his way around the table to stand before me. He is a taller man; over 6 feet with a slender build. I would guess him to be somewhere in his mid to late thirties. Garbed in a clean, white lab jacket, this man, labeled 'Doctor' by the guttural speaking man, has delicate looking features that I was not expecting of someone holding a captive. He had neatly combed, short blonde hair; was cleanly shaven; and smelled of the aftershave that I had detected earlier. Unfortunately, it was this man's aftershave smell that was also accompanied by that smell of death that still lingers in the air from when he first entered the room. He leans forward toward me and an uncomfortable feeling comes across me.

"You're safe," he whispers into my ear. I feel compelled to respond.

"Where am I? What is this place?"

"All in good time, Edward. All in time. For now, let's get you out of these restraints shall we?"

The doctor steps back to the wall behind him and opens up a panel located above the stainless steel counter. I see several little knobs and flashing buttons inside. He proceeds to press one of those buttons. Suddenly I hear a whirring sound accompanied by the sound of loud clanging, and the leather straps binding my arms and wrists begin to loosen. My legs too, begin to feel pressure being relaxed, as straps begin to loosen from them as well. The doctor then reaches behind me and I feel his movement as he un-clips a buckle from a strap that runs across my lower back. Then, in an instant, I am free.

I jump from the table, still dripping of blood from the pool that I had been lying in, and quickly grab the soft-spoken doctor by the throat.

"You will explain everything to me. NOW!"

I loosen my grip just enough to allow him to speak.

"I… I can't do that," the doctor said. "You must understand… you are needed, but I can't explain it all to you now. We must get you out of here. The longer we delay…"

His words are cut short as the lights suddenly go out. Then, from the far wall, a blinking red light be-gins to flash much like a strobe.

"What's happening?" I shout, as my grip instinc-tively tightens once again about the doctor's throat. He gasps for air; I comply with the loosening of my fingers.

"It's too late. You must go. You must not get caught."

He points to a strange-looking instrument on the counter and then waves his finger upward to the panel on the wall above.

"Take that and then press the green button. It is very important. Now go. Outside the door, you'll see a jacket. Take it and go."

Not exactly understanding the situation I am in, but understanding that this may be my only opportunity for escape, I release the doctor's throat. Feverishly, I grab the unusual device from the counter that the doctor had pointed out to me. I then press the green button which I can hear immediately unlocks the large silver door, and I make my way for the exit. As I open the door and look for any sign of a direction to go, I grab the spare lab jacket hung just outside the door as the doctor had mentioned it would be. I turn once more in the doctor's direction, and as our eyes meet, I think I catch a glimpse of hope in his demeanor, as he undoubtedly can see the unspoken 'thanks' in mine. I look back out at a darkly lit hallway with the same blinking red lights flashing overhead, and then I vanish from the doorway opening. As I head down the corridor running as swiftly as I can for a man in my condition, I think I hear a brief, ominous message come from the doctor's lips.

"Save us!"

Chapter 3

The Good with the Bad

One thing that strikes me as unusual, as I roam from one dark corridor into another, is that although there is a flashing strobe of red with every turn I make, it has not been accompanied by any sort of audible alarm. I had assumed that the sudden blackout followed by the red lights was some sort of acknowledgment that my actions toward the soft-spoken doctor while held in that room had been scrutinized. He did, after all, make mention of a camera that had been on the wall behind me. Adding to my assumptions was the doctor's words warning me of not getting caught. And of course, the last words I heard spoken from him... "Save us." Funny words really, spoken to a man held captive, confused, half beaten to death, and on the run. How can I be expected to "save us," whoever "us" refers to, when I can't even find a way to save myself? Furthermore, "save us" from who, or from what? My mind right now is in the dark as much as my body has been for some time. "Save us," the doctor said, but the only thought that keeps coming to the forefront of my brain right now is "save me."

Even more suspicious is that I have not come across a single person since I escaped the surgical room. I left that place wearing only a pair of blood-soaked white shorts and a white lab coat that I can only assume was left for me outside the room by the doctor. I find myself barefoot, clinging to the walls of each pathway I choose in this never-ending labyrinth of left and right turns, leaving a trail of blood droplets behind me as I make my way to... where? I have no idea where I am or where I am going. I feel the burning in my back beginning to renew. There are puncture wounds on the inside of my forearm that suggest I was most likely given something intravenously to minimize the pain from the lashings that I had received. Unfortunately, the returning waves of pain, and the excruciating burning sensation I feel, suggests that the effects of whatever medication I was given are wearing off.

Have I been going in circles? Since I left the doctor in the room where I lay captive, I have been following a series of narrow, non-descript hallways. Each hallway of white painted brick construction, having no distinguishing features from the last, seems to adjoin to another narrow white hallway that leads me to yet another. There have been no doors; no windows... nothing, save for the red flashing lights above that guide my way. Their ever continuous intermittent bursts feeding my senses; three seconds on, two seconds off, as I pass under a new flashing light every ten paces or so. The cold, hard tile floors beneath my feet make it easy to notice how shaky my legs feel. How long have I been walking? Has it been five minutes or an hour? I'm getting tired. No doubt it is from a combination of the loss of blood, the pain medication, and from the extended time spent in that dark, confined space that I called my home for so very long. I need to rest for a moment to gather my strength before I collapse.

As I bend over to place my hands on my knees to help stabilize them, I feel the lab coat, which had since stuck to the wounds inflicted on my back, rip clean from the flesh. I want to scream out, but I know that to do so would surely lead to me being captured once again. I clench my teeth and breathe in a heavy breath. Wounded, confused, tired, I look back at the trail of blood on the tile floor that clearly shows each not-so-subtle move I have made to this point. I close my eyes for a moment and my mind wanders... back...

"Eddie. Yo Eddie, my man. You dog, you. Is that the waitress you've been scouting?"

Travis Wehring, a private first class, who managed to find his way into becoming a roommate of mine after his other three roommates couldn't make it through basic training, was always quite direct.

"Shhh! Keep it down Travis. I'm not 'scouting' anyone. I have a girl."

Of course, these words are leaving my lips as I find myself peering down to the other end of the alcohol-laden bar, staring at the sultry brunette delivering a drink to a mumbling boozer who looks like he's had about ten too many.

"Yeah, you've got a girl back home... but you're not home."

Along with being direct, Travis also had a knack for stating the obvious. He wasn't the brightest bulb for sure, but he was a good friend, and he stuck by you. He was a big ox of a man; all muscle, but kind-hearted to a fault at times. We had gotten to know each other pretty well once he was assigned the bunk below me some months back.

"You know, Travis, I come to this bar to get away from it all, not to be reminded of what I can't have." I pause for a moment. "She is hot though isn't she?"

A smirk runs across Travis' face.

"Oh yeah buddy, you know it. So what are you going to do about it?"

"Nothin'. I just like to look is all. Nothin' wrong with that."

"Nope," Travis agrees. "Nothin' at all."

We clang glasses together to toast another week of surviving the grueling pressures of the military and spend the rest of the evening talking about home, the future, the attractive waitress, and other non-important things that seem to make their way into our conversation. It's a good night. A good night, that is, until we decide to leave.

As we make our way out into the parking lot, I fumble for my keys in my jacket pocket, as the ef-fects of the alcohol begin playing tricks on my fin-gers. Not fully aware of my surroundings, I neglect to

notice the two men approaching from behind me and
Travis. Before either of us can react, I am immediately struck in the head with something hard that sends
me down to the ground onto my stomach. I manage
to turn slightly to see Travis being struck behind the
knees with a tire iron that drops him to the ground. I
try to get up but can't make it to my feet. I feel a
warm stream of blood as it washes down into my
eyes. I grab for my head and feel a large gash that
makes me believe that I must have a skull fracture.
Unable to react to anything at that moment, I glimpse
a flash of light coming from the edge of a knife
wielded by one of the assailants. In an instant, it is
too late. The knife is plunged into the side of Travis'
neck down to the handle and then yanked out violently, causing blood to spray in every direction as his
head convulses back and forth uncontrollably. I immediately scream out in horror. The two men run off,
never looking back to see the results of their unpro-
voked, malicious attack. I hear gurgling sounds coming from Travis as he lay there in a pool of blood, his
neck still releasing large amounts of fluid.

"Hang on Travis," I begin to yell. "Hang on. Oh
God, hang on man."

I try to make my way over to Travis' still, lifeless
body, but I can't seem to get my legs to work. I begin

to crawl toward him; every movement I make is excruciatingly painful due to the injury I have sustained. I reach out for him, but I never make it before everything fades away to darkness.

I open my eyes back to my present reality. I convince myself that I need to focus if I'm ever going to get out of here. I must get back to the task at hand. I straighten up, look back once more at the trail of blood droplets from where I came, then look forward in the direction calling me onward. I take a step, then another, then another again. I know my body is weak but my mind keeps yelling at me to keep going. My mind wins. My pace begins to quicken, as once again I find myself leaving one darkened corridor behind me, and facing another darkened corridor ahead of me. The flashing red lights still flickering on and off, three seconds, two seconds, on and off, causing a dizzying feeling in me that may be partially responsible for my wobbly legs, as I make my way down this most recent hallway.

As I stumble to make my way to the end of this current passageway, the blinking red lights suddenly cease to blink; becoming instead a solid glow of red lighting the way. This presents an eerie feeling that sends a chill down my spine. I continue making my way to the end of this hall, which I can see up ahead, leads to a right turn. I can only imagine it is going to be just another path in this series of mazelike corridors I have already traversed. I peer cautiously around the corner as I have done around each such corner I have come to, and I am suddenly filled with a feeling of shock as much as relief. The hallway that opens up before me is much the same as all the ones previous, except that this one ends with a door located at the far end. I can feel my heart race faster, and perhaps even jump up into my throat. I slowly, cautiously take the first step toward the door with my right side pressed firmly against the corridor wall. I stop for a second, glancing back once more at the blood on the floor that looks more like a trail I have been following rather than a trail that has been following me. I see the streak of crimson that my back has left as a message on the wall behind me, and then look forward toward the door ahead of me. Without another thought I run as quickly as I am able, feeling a pulsating pain shoot through my back with every heavy footstep that lands on the unforgiving floor beneath me. I pay it little attention as my goal lies ahead of me.

I reach the door and can hear a slight humming sound coming from the other side. I hesitate briefly as I reach for the knob of the entryway before me. I know not what is on the other side of this door. I pause, deciding to instead put my ear to the door to listen. For about a minute, my ear is pressed firmly against the door, and for that minute all that is heard is a continuous humming sound. I hear no voices, no movement… nothing else. I reach down for the knob again, grip it tightly with a sweaty palm and slowly begin to turn it hoping that it is not locked. I don't think I have the strength to try to break it open. Thankfully, the knob turns freely. As I slowly open the door, the red lights that have been my only source of sight since I left the surgical room, suddenly go out leaving me in complete darkness.

I am left here holding the door open but unable to see what lies in front of me. I notice that the humming sound that was emanating from beyond the door has also now ceased. It is quiet. Quiet and dark. I can feel my heart begin to race. Each beat causing a surge of pain to erupt from the wounds inflicted upon my back. My hands have already started to quiver. I bring them up to rub my eyes to see if that will help me refocus. My body slumps sideways and comes to rest on the frame of the doorway. I stand frozen for a moment, trying to relax my nerves, my hands still pressed firmly against my eyes. Once settled, I lower my hands from my face, but the darkness remains. I look back behind me to see the same blackness. Do I go through the door? I do not know where I am. I don't know where this new threshold leads. All around me is encompassing darkness. I gaze forward into the doorway, and then I gaze back to the direction I came from. My mind is racing to determine what the right answer is. I think for a moment, and then a sudden calmness comes over me. In an instant, the decision comes to me ever so clearly. I know the hallways behind me. I know what the plain brick walls and blood-stained floor could easily lead me back to; nothing. There is nothing back there but a cold, dark room that once held me captive. Ahead of me is the unknown for sure. But with that unknown comes a chance; a chance of something else; a chance of hope. And so, with that thought resonating in my brain, the decision becomes much clearer than what my eyes presently show me. I step through the doorway.

Chapter 4

Persona Non-Grata

If hope is what I'm looking for, it sure has a nasty way of playing Hide and Seek. Since I decided to step sight unseen through the unlocked door, I was convinced it could lead me out of this miserable hell-hole I'm in. Instead, I've done nothing but feel around in the dark in hopes to come across something my hands might recognize. Thus far, I've managed to locate a wall. It's not made of brick, like the walls in the endless maze outside the door that led me here. This wall is smooth to the touch. As smooth as glass. The floor is still cold though. As hard as it is to concentrate, with the constant burning sensation coming from my back, I can still feel the cold. Why couldn't the doctor have left me some shoes to go along with the lab jacket?

Why are the lights still out? Why did they go out, to begin with? I can't believe that the entire place, whatever this place is, is in the dark. Why is there no one around? Besides the cigarette smoking, guttural sounding man and the soft-spoken "doctor," there has been no sign of anyone, anywhere. No time to think about that now. I've got to keep feeling around. There's got to be something. My hand slides across the smooth surface of the wall that I have momentarily rested on. I forget which way is forward and which way is back. It's amazing how disoriented one can become when surrounded by total darkened emptiness. If I follow this wall it will lead me somewhere, won't it? So I walk, keeping my left hand sliding along the smooth wall, while my right hand frantically waves in scattered motions in front of me to interact with any obstacles or walls that I may come across.

More minutes pass before I begin to think this is a lost cause. This is very strange. Surely I should have come across something by now. There has not even been a single breakage in the smooth plane about which my hand has been careening across. This whole place is very strange. One minute I'm in my dank, dark sanctuary wallowing in self-pity, drudging up old memories to keep me sane, the next I'm being delivered into a bright light and beaten and whipped to unconsciousness. I then find that I've been strapped down to a table and who knows... maybe experimented on, only to be let loose and told to run and escape so that I can save... someone. I just don't get it. There must be something I'm missing.

I try to collect my thoughts for a minute to discern what has happened. The doctor... he said I was "safe," that I was "needed." What else? Think Edward! What have you learned? Think back to where you were lying on that table pretending to be incognizant when the two men entered. What were their words? The harsh voiced man had asked the doctor if I would work. He wanted "no mistakes this time." So there were others? Am I a mistake? Or was the mistake me listening to the doctor in this feeble attempt to escape? Perhaps this was all part of his plan; to set me free to see what I would do. That would explain why there has been no one that I can tell who is even remotely concerned with my escape from that room. Am I just a big mouse in a maze searching out my piece of cheese? I know my mind may be groggy, and I am not at all at full capacity by any means, but how can I have fallen so easily for a ruse that even a child could have picked up on? I do not have my wits about me, of that I am sure. Something else I am quite sure of is that I have been walking for several minutes on this seemingly singular straight plane with no sign of an end. I have had no interaction of any kind to any other object except for this damnable never-ending surface that has served no purpose to me except to have helped support my weight as I feel myself becoming weaker.

I stop once again and feel a bead of sweat trickle down the crease of my nose before coming to rest softly on my lips. The taste of salt briefly renews my senses and I feel a similar trickle of liquid make its way down my back. That, though, is most assuredly blood. I hunch forward just a bit and feel the rear of the lab jacket act like a sponge as it softly caresses across my back. At that moment, a decision is made. I straighten myself back up, drag my right hand down my face to remove any remaining condensation that has since started to form, and then, taking in a deep breath, I push myself away from the wall that has been my guiding resource since I made my way into this room.

Turning ninety degrees to my right so that my back is toward the wall, a quick thought enters my mind that this could be a big mistake, but then just as quickly subsides as if the thought was never there at all. I lumber forward a few steps cautiously, not knowing what lies in front of me; all the while my arms once again dancing in waves of circular motions ahead of me much like an insect's antennae are used as feelers to ascertain information about their surroundings. No sooner do I make my way about five feet from the wall when suddenly the room is cast in full incandescence. My pupils immediately constrict causing me to instinctively cover my eyes with my hands. For brief seconds I am frozen in place, sharply blinded by the unexpected flash of light. Then, slowly, I begin to remove my palms from my eyes which continue squinting tightly as they try to focus and adjust to the surrounding brightness.

"Who's there?" I shout out, knowing full well that my actions are undoubtedly being watched as part of some experiment or psychological examination. I get no response.

With the blurriness finally departing from my eyesight, I look straight ahead to see an expansive, brightly lit room with nothing but surrounding emptiness that appears to have no end. I glance to both my left and right and see the same thing; a floor and ceiling that, for as much as I can tell, extends beyond my vision. My mind races with nervousness. Didn't I just come from that direction? Surely I have not walked so far; especially in my current condition; that I can't even begin to see where I once entered this room.

I turn to face the wall behind me that has been the only comfort in an otherwise uncomfortable and peculiar place that I find myself in. To my surprise, the wall in which I followed to my current location; that which was as smooth as glass; was in fact, just that... glass. It is a mirror to be more precise, which spans from floor to ceiling and also extends in both directions for as far as the eyes can see. On the floor in front of this great mirror is the familiar path of crimson that has spotted the floor behind me in a trail that now seems to go on forever. I shift my vision back to the mirror and commit my full attention to the figure staring back at me.

There I am, unclothed, wearing only the blood-red stained shorts that had at one time been white, and the loose-fitting lab coat that also has numerous patches of red about it. The jacket hangs open from my shoulders exposing my thin, malnourished midsection. I can count every rib as easily as if they were outside of my chest. My legs also appear to have fallen into a state of atrophy. Where once was muscle showcased in a body full of strength and vigor now resides a withered, sad shell of a being. Shifting my sight slightly upward to the sullen visage peering at me with hollow, sunken eyes, it occurs to me that I hardly recognize this man standing before me. I stumble forward, keeping notice of each movement this lethargic body makes as I lean into the mirror to get a closer look at this young man turned old. I know I had been in that dark, confined place for some time, with little food or drink, and even less activity to keep myself in healthy shape, but I never dreamed I had lost so much of myself.

As I stare in initial shock at my reflection, I find my thoughts scrambling to unite my current circumstances with some semblance of logic. This place, this very situation I find myself tangled in, defies all principles of common sense. Truly, a room that seems to be endless in all directions save one, and that one of which is comprised of a mirrored wall that spans infinite in length is beyond reason. A glaze comes across my blank stare, and ironically, given my current location, I reflect on the past...

"James, are you sure you gotta do this?" I asked of my brother with a heavy heart as he took another stride toward the door to exit.

He was leaving for the Gulf in the morning and he had to get back to the base. He had already said all his goodbyes to everyone he knew. From Mr. Sloan, who I'm pretty sure my brother threatened about trying to make any advances toward our mother, to Mr. Gradie, who he had looked up to during his employment at the bank. I think there was a night when my brother even bumped into Troy Thompson, his boyhood rival, and greeted him with a handshake and said goodbye. Mom and I were the last on his list.

"Sorry, little brother, I've got no choice," James replied to me. "I have my orders. But don't give it a thought. I'll be back before you know it."

Those were the words he used the first time he left, right after he quit his job at the bank. Truthfully, he liked his job tremendously, so when about eight months ago he gave his notice and surprised everybody about his decision to join the army, it shocked us all.

"I'll be back before you know it."

The words echoed in my ear. Though the first time it was true, he came back to visit a few times when he was on leave, this time felt altogether different. This time he was going off to war, and as much as you wanted to look positive and show how proud you were, there was still that thought that this may be the last time you see each other. I launched myself at him with my arms already extended, and in reciprocation, James grabbed hold of me and squeezed me close into him.

"Be careful over there," I said as I let a tear spill from my eye. "You know how mom can't take bad news."

It was a comment meant to lighten the mood as I could feel the flood gates about to open and I was going to break down in a fit of uncontrollable crying. I released my grip from him and shoved him back a bit. James knew what it was for, and simply acknowledged with a smile.

Then, as he turned to walk out the door, he glanced back one last time.

"Take care of mom while I'm away," he said. Then he was gone.

Mom was in her bedroom trying desperately to keep herself composed. James had already had his long goodbye with her before she began exhaustively weeping. She then gave him a tender kiss on the cheek and ran off to her room. After James had left, I went to her to see if she was all right. I peered in from the bedroom doorway and saw that she was sitting on the edge of the bed, with a photo album on her lap, flipping through the pages.

"Mom?" I quietly spoke, wiping tears from my cheeks.

She looked up at me for a moment with a hint of contentment in her eyes.

"Come over here, Edward. Sit with me." She tapped the bed beside her.

I walked over to where she was and sat beside her with my shoulders slumped downward and my arms crashed like lead weights onto my lap. She reached over and wrapped one arm around me and then pulled me in close as she leaned her head against mine.

"Your brother will never know how proud I am of him," she said. "I'm so very proud of both of you. You boys have always been my angels."

We sat together for most of the night, looking through pictures, talking about younger days, and consoling each other. We connected that night as mother and son more than we had done for many years before. And it felt... nice.

Presently, staring back at myself in disbelief, my thoughts are abruptly cut short as a loud, ringing voice pierces the silence.

"Sit down," it announces.

Startled by the suddenness of sound, I jump back from the mirror. I look up at the ceiling in what I believe is the direction that the voice that I heard came from. I see no speakers or open areas from which it could have come from. Then, once again, the voice rings out its demand.

"Sit down, Edward!"

The words are loud and clear and seem to come at me from all directions. I turn to look behind me and I am startled to see a small square table situated not five feet from me. At the far end of the table, facing the mirror is a chair. These furnishings had not been there before. Or were they, and this just adds to my suspicions that I have been drugged? Or perhaps the table and chair are not there in front of me at all, and they are just a hallucination brought on by the effects of the drugs that have quite possibly been administered to me? Nevertheless, my curiosity takes control of my actions and I slowly make my way over to the articles of furniture that now appear before me. Hesitantly, I reach out with my left hand to feel for the hard surface that I know in my mind can't be there. But, as this day has surely proven, strange things are indeed afoot, and the table, as unbelievable as it is, is real to the touch.

"Come now, Edward," the voice chimes again. "Don't keep us waiting. Please sit."

Looking all about me, I once again can't distinguish where the voice is coming from. Feeling that I have no other recourse; after all, there is nothing else around me but a seemingly limitless surrounding, and being that the table and chair are real, I sit.

For what feels like minutes, the room is silent as if there never was a voice. The pace of my heart quickens with anticipation of the silence being broken by the thunderous vocalization that I had heard just moments before. I decide to take the initiative.

"What do you want of me?" I yell out.

"Of you… nothing," is the reply. "But you have something we need."

"Who are you?" I demand. "Where am I?"

"That does not concern you. Give us what we need."

"I have nothing," I shout, looking all around me to detect the direction of the voice.

"You do, Edward. It is in your presence, and we will have it."

"I don't know what…" I stop for a moment, and then it comes to me like so many of my other memories. It is with me, indeed, although I had forgotten it. When I was back in the room with the doctor, he asked me to take the instrument that was atop the counter. When I had put on the lab jacket, I had placed the item in the pocket, and in the following course that I had been set on, forgot about it. It was with me all the time. I reach down into the pocket of the jacket that now hangs about my side, and I feel the instrument of which must be the item being spoken of. I pull it out in front of me and quickly begin to study it.

It is an unusual thing for sure. It is a crude-looking device; no bigger than a television remote control. Its shape is oblong, with little nubs protruding at each end. It is smooth and cold to the touch, and by sight appears to be mostly made of a type of metal of sorts, except for the protruding nubs which are like rubber and distinguishable by different colors.

"This is what you want isn't it?" I quickly stand from the table and raise the item toward the mirror as if it is from there that the voice emanates.

"Yes, it is," says the voice. "Now leave it on the table and remove yourself from here at once."

I am slightly confused by that last statement. If there is a way to remove myself from this odd place I am in, I have not found it. I reply.

"How do I leave? This room stretches to beyond my sight and I have yet to come across a means to exit."

"Behind you is the door," the voice clamors out.

I quickly look back in disbelief, but again, as if from out of nowhere, there is now a wall about twenty paces behind me with but a single door centrally located to my current position. I turn back to face the mirror and I am stunned to see that the mirror shows me no such wall. The table and chair are visible in the reflected image, that much I can clearly see, but nothing else. I look behind me once more in doubt that I saw what I saw, and of course, the wall is there. After all the day's events, I should know better than to think that anything I encounter will or should make any sense to me. This is beyond my scope of thought or reason.

"Now leave the device on the table and go," rings out the voice in a sterner manner.

In a defiant tone, I reply, "And if I don't?"

As if noting my defiance, the mysterious voice seems to rise in volume and temperament.

"You should not ask a question for which the answer will not be to your liking. You have but an easy task before you and yet you still question us with insubordinate speech. Do you not understand, after everything we have allowed you to see? You are nothing to us; insignificant. We need nothing of your being save that device you hold in your hand. You are neither wanted nor welcome in here any longer. Now leave the device on the table and leave at once, lest you find out the answer to your question."

Having never been one to back down, but feeling my current situation is beyond me, I choose the better part of valor. I drop my chin to my chest and look down again at the object I hold in my hands. I don't know what it is or how it is used. I don't know why it is so important to whoever it is that is running this show. Whatever it is, it was important enough for the doctor to want me to take it with me. Maybe this is what I am supposed to do. Maybe the plan was to have me deliver the device to this place, to give it to this figureless voice that rings out like the '*Great and Powerful OZ.*' And why can't it be for that reason? It is the only thing that makes sense; if sense is what you can call it. And so, with the means of escape shown to me, and my eagerness to want to leave this place, I slowly rest the strange device on the table in front of me. I begin to pull the chair aside, and without much thought, I mutter one final comment to state my acceptance of the request that was asked of me.

"It's all yours, *'OZ.'*"

And at that moment, it hits me. The character in the book... that particular character; *The Wizard*, was thought to be a wondrous, great, and powerful being of which whose tremendous voice commanded respect from his many followers, but whose true identity instead, was nothing more than a little man hiding behind a curtain. It was all a ruse. And so too, I suddenly believed, was this; and I would like to have a peek behind the curtain.

With my hand still clutching the chair, I feel my grasp tighten. Then, without a moment's hesitation, I grab it with my other hand and fling it with as much force as I can muster toward the mirrored wall. For the briefest of moments, time seems to stand still. Then in an instant, the sound of shattering glass fills the emptiness. I turn away to avoid any shards that might find their way showering in my direction. It was then that I notice the door, the very same door that I had been led to believe was to be my exit to freedom, vanish before my very eyes. Simultaneously, walls come into view all around me joining with the once, great wall that had displayed my reflection. It seems what appeared to be an expansive landscape of nothingness was just a clever illusion cast upon a simple room with plain white brick walls, similar to those that led me to this chamber in the first place. The chair that I had launched in skeptical defiance has pierced the very heart of this grand façade and was now showing me beyond the wall for which I stared at in reflective thought minutes before the voice clamored. Gazing through the gaping opening of shattered glass that now stands before me, and faced with the sudden realization that 'OZ' was just a farce, one simple thought enters my mind; *"There's no place like home."*

Chapter 5

The Man Behind the Curtain

Every once in a while, in moments like this, a calmness washes over me just to let me know that a storm is coming. As I stand in silence in this room that was not a room mere moments ago, I can't help but wonder what the great plan is. What is this all about? It has become obvious to me that I was purposefully led here to this room. I was almost tricked into leaving behind the strange device which I carried here in my pocket, although I had forgotten about it for a time. The great voice that rang out earlier demanding the object from me almost had me believing that this was some incredible, fantastic place that no man was ever supposed to set eyes upon. I was instructed to forsake the object, despite what the doctor said if I was to leave from the room. Had I not done what the voice commanded, I was going to find out what horrible things would be done to me for disobeying my supposed captor. Luckily I came to my senses in time, with a little help from distant memories of a children's story.

Having broken the large wall of glass in front of me, I peer in with squinted eyes to see naught but a bunch of colorful, flashing lights penetrating an otherwise pitch-black room. I look down on the floor where I am standing and notice the trail of blood that had been dripping from my back since making my way into the maze-like hallways. The scene shows me a different picture altogether. What I saw as hallways leading me to where I currently stand has now been revealed to me that I have instead been following the perimeter of this room. It appears that I have been going around in circles over and over, with the occasional detour across the length or width. Do my eyes deceive me? How is it possible that I am in the same room? Where did the hallways go?

There is suddenly a horrible feeling building up inside of me that tells me I have absolutely no idea what is real around here anymore. I now know that I cannot trust my eyes, but what about my ears, or any other senses for that matter? The pain searing from my back certainly feels real, and the trail of blood only reinforces my belief that it is. I'm just not sure what to believe anymore. I've already learned that what I think I see may instead be completely different than what is shown before me. How do I know the pain I feel isn't just a false sense of feeling that my mind has been tricked into thinking is real?

Another thought that enters my mind is how it is that I came into this room, to begin with. I know… well, I think I was in another room; the surgery room, with the doctor, and that I stepped out of that room to enter what I thought was the system of passageways that led me to the entrance to this room. If that is true, then where is the door? There is nothing around me but three walls of brick and a shattered wall of glass. I decide not to think too much about it at this time and concentrate instead on the darkened room that has now been revealed to me from beyond the glass. I am not keen on the idea of going back into another dark room, not knowing where I am or where I am going, but there is nothing left for me in this lighted room anymore. I turn back to the table that stands in the center of the room and I retrieve the odd device that I placed on it. I put it back into the lab coat pocket where I had pulled it out from, thinking to myself that this time I will remember that I have it, and I turn once again to face dozens of small flashes of color coming from the blackness beyond the mirror. If I am going to find a way out of this crazy funhouse, it will be through there.

Cautiously, I make my way over to the newly created opening in the wall, being careful not to step on any shards of glass that have carpeted the floor. The last thing I need right now is to have my feet fall into the same condition my back is in. Once at the opening to this new room, I feel with my foot that there is a step-down, but I do not know how big of a step it is, and with no light to guide me, I have no way of knowing the whereabouts of all the glass that must be scattered about the floor below. I squat down low to the ground and sit at the entranceway and slowly bring my feet down to catch the lower floor of the black room. The lower floor is about a foot below where I am perched, and having felt that my feet are not touching any glass, I stand up out of the lighted room and into this new dark place. Still not being able to see anything clearly except for the blinking reds and yellows and blues that strobe on and off in random patterns in front of me, I have to slowly slide one foot after the other across the floor to prevent injury from the broken glass that I can feel strewn across the floor. About five paces in from where I first stood up, the lights suddenly turn on revealing a small room, square, about twelve by twelve, filled with computers and control panels along each side wall, each having multiple sets of the colorful blinking lights which accounted for the only thing I could see when I first looked in. Straight ahead of me on the far wall, there is a steel door that I can't help but think, if I am to step through it, will undoubtedly only lead me to another place of mystery. On the same wall in the right corner near the ceiling, there is a motion sensor that I can only speculate to be the reason behind the lights coming on as it detected my movement. Opposite the sensor, in the left corner of the room, I notice a video camera that lets me know I am still being watched. To the left of me lies the chair that I used to create the large jagged threshold, and in essence, reveal to me the false reality that I had been stuck in. This room must serve as some sort of control room that is used to create the illusions that I witnessed in the previous area. What is the purpose of such a room, and why the trouble of so elaborate a hoax? And of course, the bigger question, why me?

Knowing the answers won't be forthcoming, I instead concentrate on the situation I currently find myself in, and the means of which I aim to get myself out. I focus my attention on the steel door that lies on the far wall in front of me. Although I don't know what is on the other side of it, I do know that it will be my escape route from this control room. And so I stride forward cautiously, but with a determined goal in mind. I glance up at the camera one last time before reaching the door and think of leaving the viewer with a few choice hand gestures to signify my anger and frustration, but decide against it. I instead feel a slight smirk come across my lips to convey a subtle message of confidence and I turn my sight once again to the large steel door before me. Just as I extend my arm to reach for the knob, the knob suddenly turns and the door kicks open a few inches. I jump back instantly fearing more about who may be entering the room in front of me than about the glass on the floor behind me. Thankfully I feel no sharp pain in my feet to worry about so all my attention is focused on the person entering the room.

At that moment, and not too much of a surprise to me, a familiar face peers in from behind the door. It is the doctor that sent me on my way from the surgical room. His soft-featured countenance appearing no different to me than it had when we first met. And then there is that same hint of aftershave and death that hits my senses from before. As the door swings fully open, I see that the doctor is accompanied by another man standing behind him. This other man is shorter than the doctor by several inches but stockier by far more. His features are much in contrast compared to that of the doctor's. He has very deep-set eyes with very large hairy eyebrows above. His nose is very bulbous with nostrils that flair immensely to each side. Pot-marked cheeks outline his visage down to a thick, cleft chin. He stands very sharply dressed in a dark suit and tie, a fitted brim hat upon his head and a cigarette stemming from his corpulent lips. This I can only assume is the other man from the surgical room that had directed the doctor to "do his part" and to "make no mistakes this time." Seeing this other man makes me feel a bit uneasy and I clench my fists tightly as I slide backward a step toward the broken mirror behind me.

"You can relax, Edward," the doctor says. "You're among friends."

I don't say a word in response, but instead, my eyes shift to the smoking man behind the doctor. This is meant to express my lack of trust for one who I have not met before. The message is understood clearly.

"Ah yes, of course." The doctor gestures behind him. "This stout gentleman is Mr. Greeg. His appearance I assure you is far more wretched than his demeanor."

"Thank you for that, doctor," the portly man states in a wheezing guttural voice, confirming my suspicions about him being the one from earlier.

"You're quite welcome, Mr. Greeg," the doctor replies with a smile on his face as he turns to face me once again.

"I'm sure you are very confused about everything right now, Edward, and I can't say as I blame you. We have put you through a rather unbelievable, yet necessary, set of circumstances. But I feel it is time now to end this charade and formally introduce myself. I am..."

The doctor extends his right hand to gesture for a handshake and I immediately grab it and yank him to me forcefully. Spinning him around to face Mr. Greeg, my left arm reaches around his neck getting him into a chokehold. Wasting no time at all, I lower myself down to reach for the floor with my right hand, the doctor's body limply following my movement, and I grasp a shard of broken glass and press it firmly against the doctor's temple as I make my way back to an upright position.

"I don't know what is going on here. I don't know who you are or what you want with me, but you're letting me out of here now or the doctor gets it." I shout toward the stocky Mr. Greeg as my right hand with the shard of glass begins to quiver.

"You don't want to do that, son," the guttural voiced man replies. "He's your only hope out of here."

The stalwart man named Mr. Greeg does not waver from his position on the floor and remains an obstacle between me and the door. Even if I were to make good on my threat and plunge my makeshift weapon into the doctor's skull, I am sure this large man would be upon me before I could make a second move. This bulky Mr. Greeg would surely be difficult to overcome even if I was in great physical shape, but in my current condition, I would be no match to stand against him.

A gurgling sound comes from the choking doctor's lips, and I ever so slightly release just enough pressure from his throat to allow him to gather up a breath of oxygen. In that brief moment, he begins to speak.

"It's all right, Mr. Greeg. He doesn't know."

The doctor puts his hands forward to motion Mr. Greeg not to advance on me. Curious of the words just spoken, I yell to Mr. Greeg.

"I don't know what?"

"You don't know who you're holding," Mr. Greeg replies.

It's true; I don't know who I am holding. Although I can swear he may have tried to tell me his name moments ago. But with the thoughts that were swirling in my head at the time, about the course of action I was going to take, it sounded mumbled or unpronounced. Earlier I thought this man to be someone I could trust or at least someone who was possibly an unwitting puppet who needed my help, and who offered me a bit of help in return. Now it seems that I was the puppet all along, and this man; this... doctor; might very well be the one pulling the strings.

"You should release me, Edward," the doctor says in a bit more stern voice.

"I'd listen to him, kid," Mr. Greeg adds. "You're only inviting trouble if you continue this course."

I know he's right, but my options are very limited at this point. I attempt one last notion of defiance and bravery in the hopes that my desperation to leave this place is so overwhelmingly convincing that the consequences that I will face if I attempt an escape and fail are small in comparison to those I face if I don't make the attempt at all. There is also the chance that the doctor's life may be more important than they're willing to take the chance with.

"I'm inviting trouble with whichever course I take, Mr. Greeg. The way I see it, if trouble's coming for me, I may as well do something deserving of that trouble. Wouldn't you agree, doctor?"

I squeeze the chokehold just a bit tighter around the doctor's neck and glare intently forward at Mr. Greeg.

"Ok Eddie," Mr. Greeg says as he takes a puff of his cigarette, "May I call you Eddie? Remember, I did warn you."

At that moment, a sharp pain, sharper than any I had felt previously, races down my back as if it were on fire. The pain is so intense that it forces me to release the doctor in one instance and then forces me to my knees in the next. Then as quickly as it came across me, the pain is gone and replaced with a cooling sensation that is incredibly soothing and exhilarating.

Still kneeling on the floor, I look up to see the doctor now standing several feet away from me, his face very stoic.

"Sorry about that, Edward, you left me no choice. I would have rather you simply let me go, although your reluctance to do so has confirmed my decision about you. You see, Mr. Greeg, I told you he is the one."

"He doesn't give in easily that's for sure," Mr. Greeg replied. "He could stand to learn some manners though."

"All in good time, sir," the doctor added, "all in good time. Now then, let's see if we can't do this a bit more civilized this time around. Are you all right, Edward? If I'm not mistaken, you should be feeling quite invigorated about now. Come, stand. It's been quite some time since anyone has knelt before me."

My mind can't help but race in all directions at once. I don't know what just happened, but the doctor is right… I do suddenly feel so very much better. The doctor keeps spouting off things that, if taken at face value, are supposed to lead me to believe that he had something to do with the sudden pain I felt that caused me to release him. It also sounds like he is trying to take credit for my sudden renewal of energy. I will admit that it was quite the coincidence that no sooner did Mr. Greeg warn me than my back flared up with such excruciating pain causing me to let the doctor go. But sometimes that's all it is; coincidence. Whatever the circumstances affecting his release, the fact of the matter is that everything seems just a bit more confusing now than it did before I was in this precarious situation. Neither the doctor nor Mr. Greeg has taken any action against me since I have been on my knees, which I guess I should be thankful for, but I still have no trust for either of them.

Taking the doctor's words under advisement, I slowly gather my bearings and anchor my legs beneath me. With more strength than I feel I've had in who knows how long, I stand up from the ground and peer suspiciously at the two men before me as if I am expecting to be struck back down to the ground as punishment for what I had done.

Still very much confused about everything, I manage to find the nerve to utter a few questions.

"What's going on here? What is this place? What do you want with me?"

The doctor's solemn expression doesn't offer any answers as I had hoped, but then I honestly didn't expect any either. He slowly looks back at the wide presence of Mr. Greeg, which is quite intimidating, and then he turns back to me with a slight hint of what I think is a smile on his face.

"I will answer your questions, Edward," the doctor relays to me, "but you must understand that this is something that is not usually done, and especially not to someone such as yourself."

I don't know that I understand that last comment; "someone such as yourself," but I can learn to overlook that if it gets me some answers. Just then I notice the doctor once again extends his right arm to gesture for a handshake. This time, thinking perhaps a different approach may be appropriate, I accept and greet him with the handshake he requests.

"Yes, nice to have you in this better manner," the doctor states. "Now, as I began to mention before, my name is Ygdarmisalenth."

Chapter 6

Interlude 1:
Everything Changes

Sarah looks down with heavy eyes and an even heavier heart at the clothes strewn about the floor of the room. All of the pictures that used to be hung nicely on the walls now lay at her feet in shattered disrepair. She's come into this "special place" every day for quite some time now. Some days she finds herself coming in just to relax and try to get away from the tedious monotony of everyday life. It has often been a place where she can sit and let her mind wander as she takes in the quiet and calmness of the morning. Other days are reserved for simple upkeep and cleaning. And occasionally there are the days that are the hardest on her, and this room serves as a place to release any pent-up anger and frustration. Sometimes the rage builds up inside of her to such a degree until it has no place to go except outward. Today has been such a day.

These instances of aggression and sudden outbursts are the closest things she has to her feeling anything anymore. They act solely as her temporary process of healing; if healing is what you can call it. She knows that she will never feel quite whole again and that sometimes these moments where she is so totally consumed by rage and violence are the only moments that allow her to cope with the decision that she must ultimately make. She has tried other methods, such as seeing a therapist, a psychiatrist, and even having several discussions with a priest; all of which seemed to serve no other purpose than to simply pass the time. She would leave each of these meeting sessions with the same feeling of angst and utter depression as when she first arrived. The medication that she was taking too, only seemed to make her ill until she could not take them anymore for fear they were causing her more harm than good. She was never too partial to the taste of alcohol, so the idea of drowning her sorrows at the bottom of a bottle never really appealed to her. Even her friends who had stood by her for a time have all faded from recent memory, no doubt from the overwhelming pressures placed upon them by Sarah's incessant needs and her sudden changes in temperament. She has all but pushed them away, feeling it necessary that she learn to deal with the situation on her own.

Thinking back to about six months ago, the decision to occupy herself and her mind by burying herself in her work seemed to be a viable option. She had always been a dedicated, hard worker. And being a contract administrator for a major government-funded healthcare organization in Washington D.C. allowed her the opportunity to work as many hours as she saw fit to keep her troubled thoughts preoccupied; however temporary that might be. After spending the entirety of each day and many more hours into the late evenings at the office, Sarah still felt the bitter sting of having to leave work each night.

The routine was all too familiar to her. Having heard no change from the prior day, she would visit for about an hour with Jackie, someone she had become quite close with over the past couple of years, before heading on her way. She did not want to arrive too early in the evening to that darkened place she called home. She had learned early on that doing so would only cause her to fall into such emotional states of atrophy. So instead, each night she elected to stop and grab a bite to eat at one of the many local eateries. The only contentment she felt by doing this was her knowing that by the time she finally arrived back at her dark, cold dwelling, it would soon be time for bed. She could finally end her time among the conscious inhabitants and hopefully escape to a dream-filled world of happiness that could help her forget the pains of her harsh reality. Unfortunately, those types of dreams very rarely entered into Sarah's fragile psyche. On most nights she found herself instead, fighting bouts of restlessness and discomfort; tossing all about her bed with thrashing limbs. She would wake most mornings to find her bed coverings in such shambles as would make someone believe that a great struggle had taken place. And in fact, it had. But it was with her damnable, internal struggles; ones that she has been forced to live with for many years now.

It was during the time that she had been putting in the extra hours at work and her contracts were being fulfilled with great efficiency that made Sarah's boss take notice of the added responsibilities that she took upon herself. And so, when the opportunity arose for one of the company's contract administrators to spearhead and oversee the development of the organization's newest facility in Coral Springs, Florida, Sarah was asked if she would like to take on this daunting task. She would be fully involved with all contract negotiations of this new facility; from planning and development, proper zoning, licensing, construction, advertising, and eventually continuing through to hiring staff.

At first, she was very reluctant to the idea at all. She had noted to her boss the great responsibility that she would be leaving behind; the circumstances behind her resistance to even travel anywhere on a short vacation; much less for an extended period for work purposes. After all, because of her current situation, being away was something she viewed as being much too overwhelming on her mind. But the organization was very persistent and determined in its decision. So after much deliberation, Sarah was assured that the utmost care and consideration would be taken to ensure that all of her affairs here would be looked after with extreme judiciousness. She would most certainly be notified of any significant changes that would warrant her return.

Even with these assurances, and the added amenities that the company offered to provide her in exchange for her acceptance to this undertaking, this was still a very big decision for her to make; a decision that would require her to think long and hard about over the next few days. And for the longer part of those few days, she thought about the challenges she has had to endure over the last six years; the hardship, the pain, the fits of rage, the awful feelings that she has suppressed inside for so long that an unbearable feeling of darkness has overtaken much of her soul. And she thought about her daily routines; her moments spent in her "special place," her visits with Jackie; taking it all under consideration. She also began to think about how maybe this type of distraction is exactly what she needed to regain some of her self. She had been so caught up in the worries and woes of her everyday life that she had not allowed herself to feel any joy or happiness for much of the past six years. Maybe it was time. Maybe getting away from the wintery streets of Washington to spend some time in sunny Florida would be the best form of healing she could hope for.

And with that thought lingering in her brain as she approached her boss on the fourth day since being offered the opportunity, she accepted. Of course, there was much preparation needed before she could make the trip. She was expected to be in Florida for approximately six months. This was the general timeframe allotted to complete each phase of the development process before the new facility was considered fully operational. She had to make sure her finances were all in order. She made the necessary arrangements with the post office regarding the delivery of her mail. She contracted with a local landscaper to upkeep the sidewalks in front of her house during the remaining winter months, and then with lawn care and other such duties during the spring and early summer. All of her contact information was given to the appropriate parties. She did not have to worry about travel or living arrangements, or of local transportation once in Florida, as those particulars were being handled by her company.

The most difficult of all her responsibilities and the one that weighed most heavily on her mind was that of her daily visits and of her time with Jackie. Obviously, these would cease for a time. Although Sarah and Jackie had now seen each other every day for the past few years, Sarah couldn't help but wonder if Jackie would still be here when she returned. She wished that she would, as Jackie was the one ray of hope that had comforted her during her many times of need. In truth, she thought that there was no reason why Jackie wouldn't still be around upon her return. But she also knew that, although before she had decided to leave for Florida things hadn't changed about her present circumstances for six years previous, it did not mean that things couldn't change for Jackie at a moment's notice.

And so, just days leading up to her departure, Sarah took a few days off from work to spend as much time as she could with Jackie just to visit and to talk and to explain her reasoning behind her decision. But those last few visits were different for Sarah in that every other time she had come, at least in the past couple of years, it truly felt like she was there to visit with Jackie and to get things off her chest and to perhaps vent a little. Even the days where no words were spoken, just being in each other's presence was enough to comfort Sarah. But in those final few days, Sarah found that her visits were instead filled with apologies and tear-filled eyes as she sat across the room from Jackie not once glancing in her direction as if she were not even there. The words she spoke, although they were not directly to Jackie in the manner in which she spoke them, she had hoped that Jackie understood the reasoning behind them and the demeanor in which they were delivered. This was one of the most difficult things that Sarah ever had to do; leaving this place for any lengthy amount of time. But she also knew that it was only temporary, and it was also necessary for her to do this for her mental health and well-being.

On the day of her trip, which was a late afternoon flight, she took the time to call many of her co-workers to say her final goodbyes, and then as the time approached, she boarded the plane to Ft. Lauderdale.

The flight was uneventful, and once in Ft. Lauderdale, a car was waiting for her at the airport to take her to her hotel in Coral Springs which was a mere thirty minutes away. She figured she would first settle into her accommodations at the hotel before setting out on her first task. She wanted to look for a bookstore. She had hoped to find a copy of a particular book that she would often read back home. Many nights before going to bed, it helped her to fall asleep. She did not bring her copy of this book along with her, deciding instead to leave it with Jackie in hopes that it would come as some comfort with her gone.

The local bookstore, a quaint little shop, proved to be an unsuccessful trip, as it did not have a copy of this particular book. When questioned about the availability of ordering this book for her, the store owner, who was an older gentleman perhaps in his mid-sixties, had looked it up only to find that it was out of print and that it would be very difficult to try to get a copy. Sarah conveyed to him that she was only in town on business, but that she would be around for the next several months. She also explained to him her unfortunate situation and her reasoning behind wanting this book. Upon hearing this, the store owner was very kindly, and he offered to contact a few other bookstores. He would try his very best to find her a copy. Sarah thanked the fine gentleman and stated that she would be back in a few days, and then she headed out into the warm evening air.

It was beginning to get late, and she decided to grab a bite to eat at a nearby café just a block or so from her hotel. It was a beautiful night, and she elected to eat at one of the tables outside that lined the front windows of the establishment. While she sat there, enjoying her meal, her thoughts wandered back home. She thought to herself how she has been gone for less than a full day and already she is tormenting herself about her decision. Right then and there, she made up her mind to stop thinking that way. Everything would be fine, and everything would remain the same even with her away. And for the first time in a very long time, Sarah felt a sudden calmness envelope her, and something that resembled a smile pierced her lips. She finished her meal and retired back to her hotel where she finished unpacking and settled into what would be her new living quarters for the remainder of her stay.

The accommodations were quite nice, and her company was gracious enough to arrange for her arrival in Florida three days before any work was to begin. This allowed Sarah the opportunity to scope out the new development site as well as familiarize herself with the surrounding area which she found to be quite pleasant and refreshing compared to what she was used to from back home. She took an afternoon to travel to the beach, which is something that she had always wanted to do but never had the possibility of doing before. She also knew that it would most assuredly be her last chance to do so because as soon as her work commitment was to begin, she would be on a very tight, fast-paced, non-stop schedule. She would need to focus all of her attention and efforts into the project if she hoped to complete everything on time. That was surprisingly the part of the job that she looked forward to the most as it would keep her mind preoccupied enough to get her through each day without worrying about things back home.

On the fourth day since her arrival, when the first day of work had begun, it was exactly how she had hoped. Between all the meetings with contractors and subcontractors, inspectors, and other town officials, she had little time to think about anything other than what needed to be done and what meetings needed to be set up next to keep everything rolling along smoothly. And finally, after what she felt was a very long and productive first day, Sarah called it an evening. She decided that before going back to her hotel she would first take a small detour to the bookstore once again to see if the store owner had had any luck locating a copy of the book she so desired.

When she entered the bookstore, the kindly store owner recognized her instantly and drew a smile as he made his way from around the counter to a small table situated just to the right of where she had been standing. She glanced down and immediately felt her heart skip as she saw before her the book that she requested, and had desperately hoped would be located. The nice gentleman explained that he was able to get this particular copy loaned to him from a library located two towns over. He had decided to make the trip to go get it himself rather than have it sent through the mail. He was very pleased to see her return as he didn't want his trip to have been for naught. He did however make it very clear to her that this book was only on loan to him, therefore also to her, and that it would need to be returned before her departure back to Washington D.C. She of course agreed and gave him a thankful hug before exiting to the street outside. Elated, she stared down for a few moments at the book she now had grasped between both hands and then pulled it in tightly to her chest. She drew a heavy sigh of relief, looked forward, and headed on back to her hotel where she finished the evening lying in bed reading that book as she had done so many times before. And it was a great comfort to her.

For the next three months, as the project was in full swing and everything seemed to be on schedule, the routine was the same for Sarah. She would dive right into her work; setting up meetings, drafting necessary contracts, overseeing all on-site construction, and everything else that took place; and then she would end each night nestled in bed reading her book before finally succumbing to sleep.

As with many things that are beyond our control and understanding, such is the case when Sarah received the fateful phone call just three months into her stay. It was a phone call that she had hoped would never come, and one that she dreaded more than anything else before. It would also change everything about the course in which she believed her life had been taking.

It was a Tuesday afternoon while Sarah was involved in a meeting with the electrical inspector at the site of the almost completed facility when her phone rang. Sarah intently listened to the devastating news coming from the voice on the other end. She immediately began to break down, and then after several minutes, hung up without realizing that she hadn't even said goodbye. She was confused and lost as her body began to tremble. She had no choice but to abandon the project and return to Washington. She contacted her boss, who upon hearing the news was completely understanding about her necessity to return, and made immediate plans for another at her company to be her replacement on the project. As she made her way back to the hotel, nothing seemed real. Even as she walked into the room, she couldn't remember how she had gotten there. She collapsed onto the floor and sobbed for several minutes before gathering enough strength to pick herself up. Guilt had overtaken her as she frantically began packing. She grabbed the last of her things and rushed out to the airport where she was fortunate enough to be able to get a ticket for a flight that was scheduled back to Washington later that night.

For the next five hours, she spent the remainder of her wait at the airline terminal trembling and with tears in her eyes. Departing wasn't coming fast enough. Sarah was unsettled, angry, hysterical, and everything was moving in slow motion. She continued replaying in her mind the phone conversation from earlier in the day. She just couldn't believe the sudden events that had happened while she was away, and she couldn't help but blame herself for being so selfish as to think that getting away for a little while was something that was a good idea, especially under the circumstances.

Eventually, the flight home was very uncomfortable and seemed much longer to Sarah than it was. She was very anxious to return even though she knew that it was for the worst possible reason. She continued to wonder if things would have been any different if she'd had stayed home, to begin with, instead of undertaking the large project from work that had her traveling abroad. At the very least, perhaps she would have seen something coming and would have been able to prevent that unfortunate change. But she knew it was much too late. She continued to blame herself with similar disparaging thoughts the entire trip home.

Her thoughts snap back to her present situation. It has now been three months since her return to Washington, and she finds herself in the room that for most people, and under normal circumstances, would bring comfort for them. For Sarah however, she finds herself surrounded in the chaos of her own making as she has allowed her emotions once again to get the better of her. This certainly isn't the first time she has lashed out at the furnishings in this "special place"; and it most likely will not be the last. Looking around at the carnage she has created, she realizes that she will be spending much of the remainder of the day cleaning this room and bringing it back to the state it was in when she first entered. The broken picture frames will be replaced with new ones that are packed up in a box in the basement. She has learned over time to keep extra frames available for just such occasions of released rage. The clothes will all get hung back up nice and neat in the closet. The bed will be straightened and made back up with its usual coverings. A new bulb will be placed in the lamp that had been knocked off of the nightstand causing the old bulb to shatter into pieces. All the broken glass from both the lamp and the pictures will be swept up and the carpet vacuumed thoroughly. Sadly, it is a routine she is all too familiar with, and given the number of times it has happened in the last three months, she is quite proficient at it.

This latest outburst comes on the heels of a decision that, although the thought of it has torn at her for quite some time now, she ultimately came to just a day earlier. She still doesn't know if it is the right decision or not, but it is one that she knows she will have to live with for the rest of her life. It is also a decision that comes to its conclusion tomorrow.

Chapter 7

Back in the Dark

I have heard some very unusual names before, but this doctor certainly has one that I can honestly claim is the strangest I have ever heard. "Ygdarm…" something. I was unsure even what nationality a name like that would be. I ask him to repeat it.

"It is Ygdarmisalenth, Edward," the doctor replies once again. "Try not to let it overwhelm you too much as there is far more than that you have not learned yet that I am sure will have a much greater effect on you than my name. In truth, what I have told you is only a shortened version of my true name,

just as 'Mr. Greeg' here is also a much more shortened version of his, although I must say that his lends
itself to a more pronounceable version that is much
more easily understood compared to my own."

"And what might that be?" I inquire.

"I suppose if I am to explain everything to you,"
the doctor says, "I may as well begin with our full
names, although I don't expect you to be able to repeat them. My given name is
'Ygdarmisalenthinoleptuforniuxym,' or
'Ygdarmisalenth' for short. My voluminous friend
'Mr. Greeg' is also a shortened version of his true
name; 'Mrgreeginthuliuptimonadisanemth.'"

I let out a short laugh in disbelief of what I just
heard. One thing is for certain, I definitely can't repeat them as he had mentioned would be the case.

"And what nationality is that?" I question. "What
language?"

"I don't think you understand, Edward," the doctor continues. "It is not a language at all; at least not
in the sense that you are referring to. It is merely who
we are. But come, you will not understand what I
mean until it is all explained to you."

He nods his head toward the open door behind
him signaling for us to take our leave from this control room. I don't know what it is that I am supposed

to understand just yet, but I must admit that the doctor's words have intrigued me enough to let my curiosity get the better of me. The doctor turns and exits out the door as Mr. Greeg steps aside and motions with his hand for me to go ahead and follow. As I cautiously make my way past Mr. Greeg in fear that this is all some sort of trick and that there will still be some attempt to subdue me once my guard is down, he leans in toward me and quietly speaks in an almost amusing manner.

"I told him to go with 'Darmis,' but he insisted on 'Ygdarmisalenth.' The good doctor can be quite stubborn sometimes."

I step out of the door and into a very familiar-looking hallway, following close behind the doctor. In turn, I feel Mr. Greeg following closely behind me. This is not helping my thoughts and I stay vigilant and keep my guard up. The long hallway in front of us stretches quite a distance and very much resembles the series of hallways that led me to the mirrored room earlier, but with the lights on, does not appear so intimidating. The doctor, stepping ever so swiftly, remains a few steps ahead of me the entire time as we travel this passage. I find myself quickening my steps trying to keep apace. A loud, continuous, thumping sound from behind me lets me know that Mr. Greeg also still follows, but in a much less graceful manner than even myself. I notice the doctor raise his right hand to point to another doorway at the end of the hall.

"It's just up ahead here," he says. "Then we can get down to it."

The doctor stops before the door and allows me to catch up. He then looks back toward Mr. Greeg who had fallen a bit behind.

"You should seriously think about losing some weight, Mr. Greeg," the doctor states. "Just imagine what the others will think of you upon our return."

Mr. Greeg lets out a defiant grumble as he finally makes his way to where we are standing in front of the door.

"Before we go any further, Edward, let me warn you that what you are about to see may be quite startling to you, perhaps unbelievable. I assure you however that it is indeed real and that in some way it may help you understand just a bit more. Are you prepared?"

I look at the doctor intently trying not to show how nervous I am. The doctor's words ringing in my head force my thoughts to wander in all directions at once and I can't help but imagine all sorts of inconceivable things that could lay beyond this door. I look to Mr. Greeg for some kind of assurance that entering through the door won't be as bad as my imagination is allowing me to believe, but all I get in return is a deep, wheezing sigh as he is still trying to catch his breath. I turn back to the doctor whose hand is already squeezed around the knob below ready to proceed onward.

"I've followed you this far. Don't stop now."

My heart is racing, and I imagine my words come out sounding much braver than my countenance must appear to the doctor.

"Yet another continued reason why I believe you to be the one we have been waiting for, Edward. Even though the fear shows on your face, you refuse to give in to it."

And with that comment, and a slight smile on his face, the doctor turns the knob and opens the door to reveal a most fantastic sight; Nothing!

My head tries to wrap itself around what it is that unquestionably lies in front of me. Or perhaps the correct way of thinking is what isn't in front of me at all. I gaze in from the entranceway at something that no words come to mind to be able to describe. There is an absolute nothingness in front of me. There is nothing ahead, above, below, or to either side. I feel my breath become shallow and my legs beneath me begin to tremble just a bit. It is all very dizzying. To catch my bearings I step back from the doorway and try to reason in my head what it must be that I see; or don't see; ahead of me. Disbelief has grabbed a hold of me just as the doctor mentioned that it would and I try to gather any logical thoughts I have to try to help explain the incredible sight before me. It must be a room much like the mirrored room from before. Of course, that's it. Just as that was all an elaborate illusion created to make me believe something was real that wasn't, so too, must this be a room of the same sort of illusion. It probably has a similar control room residing somewhere just beyond the entrance.

I close my mouth, which I have suddenly realized has opened in sheer awe at the spectacle of the nothingness of the room just shown to me, and look toward the doctor in hopes that he has not noticed. I try not to give away any indication of my frustration or confusion, but my words don't cooperate.

"Is this some sort of joke?" I inquire. "Am I supposed to believe this is real?"

"But it is real, Edward," returns the doctor.

"You mean like the whole illusion room back there, with the mirrors?" I question with doubtful defiance. "Come on already, I've been through this. I know how you've tried to convince me of things being real, and I know now I can't believe anything is anymore. So let's stop playing these mind games and tell me something truthful, or just bring me back to the black pit that you first pulled me from."

At that point, I feel Mr. Greeg's presence as he moves slightly closer to me from behind before the doctor raises his right hand and waves him off.

"Now, Mr. Greeg, don't be so impatient," relays the doctor, as the portly Mr. Greeg takes a step back in unspoken obedience. "You have to understand that Edward has never experienced anything like this before and that it is only reasonable that he would question and doubt these things that are not easy for someone to comprehend."

My attention shifts back and forth between Mr. Greeg standing behind me and the doctor who stands in front of me still clutching the knob of the door. I lean forward just a bit to get another glimpse of the void that appears to me just beyond the opening of the doorway. For in truth, although I know this to be some fantastic, yet fake presentation being displayed before me, it is also something of which is so completely dazzling to the eye that I can't help but want to feed my wonderment by gazing upon this amazing sight once more. As I do so, the doctor speaks…

"Careful, Edward. That is not a place you want to be in. Not yet anyway. I am merely showing this to you so that you might understand."

"Understand what?" I question, as I straighten myself up and peer back at the doctor with the full commitment of my attention.

The doctor continues. "As I stated to you moments ago, this is in fact, quite real. What you see before you, although incomprehensible as it may seem, is more real than you can imagine. Even behind you, back in the room with the mirror; which if I may add was quite brilliant of you to shatter to find your way out of; that was quite real as well. I would have expected you to simply use the door to make your exit. It was so graciously provided to you after all. Alas, it does not matter, as you would have ended up in the same place you find yourself now."

"It would have been a lot less messy though," Mr. Greeg chimes in as a slight grin pierces his otherwise stern features.

"True enough," the doctor adds, "But then it wouldn't have been as much fun now would it? After all, who wouldn't want to have a piece of glass pressed to their temple as their very breath is being choked from them? It keeps me... amusingly grounded."

A guttural laugh is heard leaving Mr. Greeg's lips before it gives way to a fit of coughing. This is no doubt brought on by years of smoking, and I assume by his sheer outward appearance, his lack of exercise. It would seem that his trying to keep up with our pace down this long hallway, although seemingly not so very long a distance as to incite such a coughing fit, has managed to take a toll on this gluttonous man.

After less than a minute, when the coughing ceases, and the large Mr. Greeg has composed himself, the doctor tilts his head slightly to the side to look past me at the now red-faced Mr. Greeg and whispers to himself, although just loud enough for me to catch the words, "It's almost time old friend."

With that remark, the doctor quickly turns his attention back to me and begins anew…

"Where was I? Right. You see, Edward, everything you have experienced thus far has been genuine and true; at least in the way in which you perceive them to be. From your time in that confined, dark dwelling, which you for some reason seemed to find comforting, to the room where you awoke and found yourself strapped to that cold, steel table. Even wandering through the labyrinth of hallways which you bravely traveled, though I am sure every fiber in your being was telling you not to continue. The mirror, the table, the chair, the computers... all of it was real. What I now show you here beyond this door; that too, is real."

"And what about the whips," I interrupt in a stern voice, "and the steel barbs that were used to rip the flesh from my back? Why were those used on me? I had done nothing to deserve that!"

"There were no whips, Edward. It was only how you perceived the pain sensation you were feeling at that moment. Your back was never ravaged or bloodied as you may have thought."

Hearing those words, I immediately and angrily reach down to grab the blood-stained jacket that drapes down from my shoulders to denounce the lies coming from the doctor's lips, only to be utterly shocked to find that the lab coat I wear has no such sign of blood on it at all. The white shorts I am wearing are also void of any crimson. In disbelief, I look back at Mr. Greeg as if to silently ask him to confirm whether the back of the jacket is blood-soaked or not.

"It's true, kid," he complies. "Your back was never injured. You just thought it was, so it was. Do you feel any pain now? Doesn't your back feel anything but torn apart?"

It does feel good in fact. Maybe it's even better than good. But I am still taken aback by all of this. It seems like nonsense. And yet it feels real at the same time. I like to think I am an intelligent person, or at least able to determine what is factual and what is fantasy. But I am having a hard time with all of this. I start to think that perhaps I am losing my grip on reality. Am I slowly slipping into madness? Have I been in the secluded darkness for so long that my mind has finally reached its breaking point and snapped? I listen on as the doctor once again begins to speak.

"I see on your face that you still can't fully succumb to the truths of that which I speak. I need to explain further, but first I think perhaps it best if you are given the chance to sit down for fear you may collapse with what I must share with you."

The doctor slowly shuts the door from which the appearance of the unforgettable nothingness has been shown to me, and no sooner does that happen than I find that the three of us are suddenly somewhere else. In front of me stands a table which looks much like the table I had sat at earlier, only that this one is accompanied by three chairs rather than just the one. I quickly try to gather my wits by learning as much as possible about my new surroundings, and as I peer behind me I am at once struck by my shocking reflection peering back at me. It would seem I am yet again back in the room with the great mirror, only that the mirror which I had shattered with the toss of the chair that currently lies beside me, is completely intact. It is also showing me a very different image of myself than what I had seen earlier. This image looking back at me is not bloody or emaciated in the least. I look down at myself to confirm and find that the image doesn't lie, at least not at this very moment anyway. I know full well that could change in an instant like so many things have so far this day. I look strong and in good health. Where once I saw pale skin that barely covered the very noticeable skeletal structure of a withered and weak man, I now see a man in great physical condition. My face also shows no sign of indented cheeks or sunken in eyes. I am seeing a much younger version of myself than what this mirror showed to me not twenty minutes earlier. I can't help but reach up and let my fingers trace around my eyes and along my cheekbones. I feel my way down my jaw to my chin as my focus begins to shift.

Just then the realization hits me that the two gentlemen here with me are casting no reflection like the stories you hear about vampires. A chill hits me causing the hair on the back of my neck to stand erect. I notice from my reflection my face becoming a little pale. The taste of salt touches my tongue from a cold bead of sweat that had dripped down onto my lips. I turn back to face the two men just as the doctor pulls aside one of the chairs from beneath the table and sits down. As if my facial features have given my thoughts away, the doctor tries to relieve me of any fear I have been stricken with.

"I assure you, it's not what you think, Edward," he says. "We are not those loathsome creatures that give little children nightmares. Come, sit down, and I shall enlighten you."

I look toward Mr. Greeg who still stands at one side of the table. He gestures toward the chair sitting closest to me and directly across from the doctor, with the meaning to encourage me to take a seat. I comply, all the while keeping my eyes glued on his every movement. Only after I am completely seated does the large Mr. Greeg speak up with a comment I am sure is meant to relax me a bit.

"I've seen what you can do with a chair kid. I just wanted to make sure you weren't going to hurl it in my direction." Mr. Greeg chuckles.

He then pulls his chair aside and heavily plants himself down nearly breaking the chair legs out from under him. As he does so, he erupts into another fit of

guttural coughing, followed by heavy wheezing noises that cause me to cringe each time he exhales. The
doctor reaches forward and takes hold of Mr.Greeg's
right shoulder in a comforting manner.

"Soon," he states.

"Heh, not soon enough though," answers back
the large man.

With the subsiding of the various noises coming
from the seemingly ailing Mr. Greeg, the doctor who
calls himself Ygdarmisalenth begins his explanation.

"This is not easy for me to explain to you in a
way that your mind is made to understand. My one
hope is that you will at least hear my words and be
open to what I tell you. It is very important to all of
us present here in this room. We who you see before
you are not at all who we appear to be. These are
merely vessels that we inhabit while we co-exist with
you on your mortal plane. And before you jump in
with any of your ignorant comments, let me reiterate
that I did use the word 'mortal' for a reason; for mor-
tals, we are not. We are angels."

"Angels??" I question, with a sneer on my face.
"Really? You expect me to believe this?"

"Believe it? No. How can you? It is beyond your
scope of reasoning. I simply ask that you listen to
what I have to say so that you might understand the

day's events and the role in which you play in all of our fates. You see, Edward, you are not the first that we have searched out. We are, however, hoping you to be the last. Whether you choose to believe it or not, we are indeed angels. That door in which I allowed you to peer into is where we are from. We had been sent here a very long time ago. Although much of our time has been spent on Earthly tasks of which there aren't any need to share, for they do not hold any pertinence to the here and now, we are ready to return home. But that door we showed you; the very one which I warned you not to get too close to for fear the urge to walk through would be too great; has become a barrier that we can only gaze through, but never pass. Had you stepped through it, it would have engulfed your very soul. That would most assuredly have been the end of our hopeful salvation. Trust me, Edward, if frustration was an emotion I was capable of feeling, I assure you it would be in knowing that our return is right there within our grasp, yet we are unable to take hold of it. It has ever been taunting us since we learned the truth of our lengthy seclusion here among your people."

With that comment, Mr. Greeg, who had, up to that point, been slouched down in his chair, suddenly props himself upright and begins to tap his fingers in a percussive manner upon the table. Ygdarmisalenth gleans from this behavior that the stout man has something to interject.

"Go ahead my friend," the doctor nods.

Mr. Greeg takes a moment to clear his throat, then turns to me and continues with this extravagant story that has thus far been presented to me by the calm doctor.

"It's like this, kid," Mr.Greeg begins. "What Darmis… uh… sorry, Ygdarmisalenth here is trying to say, is that we were sent here for a particular pur-pose, one which we didn't accomplish, and because of that we've been kinda stuck here looking for a way to get back home. We believe you might be it. And whether you like it or not, the good doctor here has made his choice, and now you're the beneficiary of that decision."

I try as hard as I can to maintain some level of se-riousness displayed upon my face but find that this has been too humorous a tale and I begin to let out a slight chuckle. As I do, I notice Mr.Greeg look to-ward the doctor with a bewildered look on his face as if to be confused by my reaction to their absurd story. How can my response be anything other than sheer laughter after the tale both these men have concoct-ed? I turn my attention to the doctor who sits across from me and see that he shows no emotion on his face. His stoic expression forces me to gather myself a bit as I can now see that these men may just be deranged enough to believe what they are spouting about. My demeanor becomes more serious as I slowly begin to sink back in my chair. Folding my arms across my chest, I cast an apologetic nod toward the man who calls himself Ygdarmisalenth.

"I do understand quite clearly your doubt in this matter," he states. "And you must surely have some questions that are eating away at you as we speak, so please, ask what you would like to know, but know that you may not like what you learn."

Complete silence is heard for the next few moments as I shift my eyes slowly back and forth between the two men sitting before me. These brief moments I use to quickly think back on the events that have so far taken place up to this very instant. A few immediate flashes in my memory trigger the first question.

"You seem to be the one calling all the shots here doctor, but back in the operating room, when you and Mr. Greeg first entered, and I was pretending to be unconscious, it very much seemed like you were the one taking orders from Mr. Greeg. What was that all about?"

"That was simply a matter of testing you," the doctor states. "I needed you to feel comfortable with me; to trust me. I needed to see how brave you could be in an impossible situation. I knew that if I could make you think that I was someone who needed your help as much as you needed mine, it would be easier for you to accept wanting to follow my instructions. As I suspected, it worked exactly as I had hoped. Despite the injured condition you were in and the strange environment you found yourself waking to, you did precisely what I had asked."

His words ring all too true. I had no idea who this man was when I first awoke, and in truth, I still have no idea, but the fact remains that I did do exactly what he advised me to do, including the subject of my next question. I reach down into the lab coat pocket to retrieve the contents I had placed within.

"Ok, you asked me to take this object from the room." I hold up the strange, oblong device that has occupied my jacket pocket since I first left the room where I shattered the mirror. "What is it, and why is it so important?"

"In actuality Edward," the doctor answers, "it's not important at all. You may be surprised to learn, it's not even real. You needed something tangible, something to give you a little push to reach your goal. I provided that for you."

"Do you not see me holding it right now?" I shout. "And yet you still try to convince me otherwise. This thing, whatever it is, is most assuredly real."

"Edward, after everything you have been through today; after that which we have allowed you to see; you still try to cling to the idea that you can determine what is real and what is not. You are strong-willed, but oh so stubborn." The doctor gestures toward his large lackey sitting to my right. "Mr. Greeg, would you please be so kind as to show our friend Edward here what it is he has been carrying about with him all this time?"

"Sure thing," Mr. Greeg speaks up as he places his left palm face-up on the table while his right index finger points to it as if to signal my response to relinquish the unique device into his possession.

"Give it here, kid," he says. "Let me show you."

I hesitate for a moment, but truthfully it is only for the briefest of moments, for I did not ask for, nor did I want this unusual instrument anyway. I place the metallic-looking object in Mr. Greeg's palm and a grin sneaks across his face.

"I love this part!" Mr. Greeg exclaims. "I so rarely get to show off. Now watch close, Eddie, this will knock your socks off… umm… if you were wearing any I mean."

Mr. Greeg raises his left hand still holding the device, and then with both arms outstretched in front of him, he holds the object lengthwise between both his palms.

"You ready for this?" he asks. "Poof!"

And with that remark, the object unbelievably, unexplainably, vanishes into thin air right before my eyes. Astounded, I push my chair back from the table about a foot, but continue to remain seated.

"You see, Edward," the doctor states. "It was never real. You needed something to believe."

I had witnessed sleight-of-hand tricks before, although this one was admittedly better than most I had seen prior. I am sure it is just another illusion cast to make me believe these two truly are what they say they are. I decide to play along with this charade a little longer, but continue to look about Mr. Greeg to see where he may have hidden the object.

"And when I was asked to leave it on the table earlier, and leave the room, what was that about then?" I ask.

"Ah yes, that. Well, you see, if you had left the device on the table as we had asked, then we would have known you were not the one we have been looking for. Anyone else would have complied with such an easy request as that which was asked of them, especially with the means of escape also shown to them in that very same room in the form of a door. But you see, Edward, you did not. And not only did you refuse to leave the object with your unknown requester, but you also did not take the opportunity to exit the room as you surely could have. Instead, you chose a much different path entirely and decided that throwing a chair through the mirror; in fact, that very mirror that now stands fully intact behind you; would be a decidedly better option than the conventional means of simply opening the door and exiting. That is when I knew you were the one to help us return."

"And how exactly am I supposed to do that?" I ask. "You're the Angels, and if you can't do it, what can you possibly think I can offer to this effort?"

"You offer much more than you know, Eddie," Mr. Greeg jumps in. "And we better think about making this happen quickly too, I don't know how much longer these vessels will hold up. I can feel mine starting to give out."

And with that, I feel I have heard enough. I stand from the chair which I have sat at patiently for perhaps too long while I listened to these incredulous ramblings.

"All right guys, this is insane. The joke's over. It's a great story, and you have shown me some neat tricks, but enough is enough. I may not know what is going on here, or what the hell this is all about, or what you are trying to achieve by making up this grand tale, but I'm not sticking around for any more of it. Show me where the door is *this* time and I'll take it."

As I begin to turn to walk away to search out the exit, Ygdarmisalenth stands from the table with his right hand raised high above his head. I pause from my departure to intently watch his movements in case I am forced to defend myself from any aggressive offense toward me. I stand and watch as his right hand slowly begins to clench into a fist, and then without warning, he slams it down onto the table eliciting a deafening, thunderous clap, followed by a shock wave that causes the floor beneath my feet to crack. Then the doctor speaks up in a tone I am at once all too familiar with. I recall hearing it previously when I disobeyed his request to leave the strange, and apparently, now non-existent object, on the table the first time I was in this mirrored room; if this is in fact, the same room.

"Sit... Down... Now!" Ygdarmisalenth shouts. "We will not be ignored, and as difficult as this may be for you, we will not be denied. We have waited much too long, and as my friend stated, our vessels are diminishing. We are in essence, in terms you can understand, dying, and I will not allow that to happen. You are the one that can help us, and you will. As I alluded to you before, it is not only ours whose fate you hold in your hands but yours as well. Lest you heed our request, I assure you that the pain you felt previously will pale in comparison to the pain and anguish that we can unleash upon you if we so desire. It is not normally our way, but if we must."

All the while this spectacle went on, Mr. Greeg did not even show any sign of flinching from his position. My ears still ringing from the slamming of his fist down upon the table, and having no reasonable explanation for how it was the doctor was able to cause the floor to crack beneath me, I heed his words and sit back down at the table beside the unflappable Mr. Greeg. As ridiculous as it may sound, I think it may be wise of me to start taking what these men are telling me a little more seriously. Could what they are saying be true? Could they be Angels? And if so, what is this threat of causing me pain? Aren't Angels supposed to be good and righteous? I have to question, if only for my sanity.

"Ok, let's say that what you are telling me is true and that I must help you or you will inflict pain upon me even worse than I felt before; I assume as a means to coerce me. Was it you who made me feel the pain previously after I was dragged from that dark hell I had been in? You say I was not whipped or beaten; that it was all something my mind just made up. Because I thought it, it was true, at least at that moment. Seeing my clothes are lacking any sign of blood confirms, if only partially, what you say. Yet Mr. Greeg here also mentioned that it was only because of the way I perceived the pain I was feeling "at that moment" that was causing my mind to create the illusion of being tortured. What was the pain then; which I was for a fact feeling; that caused the false perception?"

Ygdarmisalenth stands before me with a stern look on his face staring down into my eyes, neither of us allowing our eyelids to blink. He takes in a deep breath, and as he exhales, I witness his expression quickly shift from what had been anger seconds before to what could be described as possibly a remorseful look. Then, in a much more calm and quiet voice, the doctor once again speaks.

"Edward, I am afraid that we have not informed you of everything as of yet. To explain it would only cause more confusion. It would be easier if we simply showed you so that you might finally realize the dire situation in which we know you to be in. Hopefully, this will also make you understand why it is in all our best interests that we must mutually work together."

Ygdarmisalenth points in my direction. "If you would please look behind you, I believe you may find some answers to the many questions that remain unanswered."

Before turning, I shift my eyes to Mr. Greeg as I see a somber look on his face. The muscle above his left eye twitches causing his eyebrow to rise as he nods his head to the left directing me to go ahead and look as the doctor has instructed me to do. I feel a trickle of sweat run down my forehead along the side of my right eye, and as I begin to wipe it from my face, I turn to look at the great, mirrored wall behind me. As before, the two men present with me cannot be seen in the reflection, but the image that appears before me is not of my own either. And as I gaze at the picture cast in front of me, I sit in shock and a feeling of utter dread tears at my soul.

Chapter 8

Interlude 2:
Decisions

Sarah lies in bed staring at the clock on her nightstand as it ticks away the seconds that with every subtle click of the hand sounds like an earsplitting eruption. She can just about time the sound with the beating of her heart. She tries to determine if she has slept at all this night. It is the same thought that has run through her head every hour since she first curled up on her mattress the night before. Not having the strength to even so much as pull the covers up over her, she has lain in this same fetal position allowing her pillow to dampen with each tear that rolls down from her eyes. Her nose, too, has fallen victim to lack of attendance as a mucus buildup has formed at the openings of her nostrils which she couldn't care to even wipe away. In her mind, nothing matters anymore. Everything that gave her purpose in this life comes to an end today, and she can't help but feel the panic take hold of her and twist her stomach into knots. The anxiety builds until she feels nauseous and she can no longer keep at bay the feeling that she is going to throw up.

She forces herself to her feet and stumbles awkwardly down the hallway toward the bathroom, leveraging herself against the wall as she strides forward to keep from falling sideways. The morning sun shines in through the skylight above guiding her way as she feels its warmth caress her swollen cheeks. The nausea is suddenly that much greater with the realization that "tomorrow" has ever too quickly turned into "today." She enters the doorway to the bathroom and feels herself collapse downward to meet the porcelain bowl; her knees slamming down against the tile floor. She doesn't feel the pain that will most assuredly come once the numbness throughout her body fades. She clutches the rim of the toilet with both arms and in an instant, she can feel her body let loose. At that moment, six years of anger; six years of frustration; of helplessness; expels from her body. Six years of utter torture and consternation; of despair; all of it is released and thrust out. She clings to the bowl that she has made friends with through many of the trying times she has felt this same way. She knows the discharge of such feelings is only a temporary relief, as they will build up in her again before too long as they always do. She cherishes these brief moments that help her to forget, if only for a few fleeting minutes.

Now that she finds herself out of bed, albeit for not the kindest of reasons, she determines that her day must inevitably begin. This will not be a typical day for her, but she tries to hold out for hope as she grasps to the notion that perhaps today, this very morning, her prayers have been answered and she will not have to ultimately go through with the decision that has all but been made for her. It's exhausting to think how her prayers have gone unanswered for so very long, and that after today, if still unanswered, there will be no need for prayer anymore.

Sarah pushes herself up from the porcelain that has been a mild comfort to her and shakily manages to gather her legs beneath her. As she does so, she catches a glimpse of herself in the mirror. What has happened to this woman, she thinks. This woman who used to be so filled with life; with love. Now the look of herself disgusts her. It is not because of the scraggly hair that has for days gone unmanaged and now hangs down with oh so many knots below her shoulders. It is not because of the blood-shot eyes that still hold remnants of the tears that won't quit or the puffy flaps of skin that have formed below them causing her to look as if she has aged twenty years in just the six. It is none of that. She knows no reason really why she holds herself in such disdain. She knows it is through no fault of her own that the decision she intends to make today has been for some time a foregone conclusion. As much as she would like to deny it, she simply can't anymore. This day was always a possibility, as was mentioned to her many years ago, whether she wanted to believe it or not. But now that a decision has been made, and the day has come for her to live with that decision, she suspects that she will no longer look at herself in the same light as she once had. It is for this reason that her reflection causes her a significant amount of distaste.

Sarah grabs for the towel that hangs from the bathroom doorknob and wipes her mouth to clear away any remnants that may have been left behind. As she flushes the toilet, she hears a subtle knocking coming from the front door. She already knows who it is, as she had made arrangements to be picked up today. She didn't feel like she was going to be in any condition to drive, especially after the deed has been done.

She sluggishly makes her way to the door, still in disbelief at how quickly the morning has forced its way into her already screwed up life. Perhaps, she thinks, that maybe this is not who she is expecting and that it is instead someone who will tell her what she has been waiting to hear for the last six years. Maybe the person on the other side of the door will tell her that everything has changed and that she no longer needs to go through with her decision. This thought quickly diminishes as she knows that any such communication would come in the form of a phone call rather than a personal visit at her home. No, this is who she expects it to be, and she also realizes that nothing has changed.

Sarah opens the door to find Jackie standing in wait, a somber look on her face, and arms outstretched signaling a wanting for an embrace. At the sight of this, Sarah once again breaks down in tears and falls forward to oblige Jackie's unspoken request.

The two stand motionless, squeezing each other intently, not wanting to be the first to relax their hold on the other. In moments it comes, however, when Sarah pulls away and composes herself to the best of her ability given the circumstances. Her hands still clenched on Jackie's arms, she tries to muster a convincing smile in acknowledgment of her thanks for her friend being there for her. Jackie smiles in return, but with eyes still showing signs of sadness.

"You don't have to do this today," Jackie reminds Sarah. "There's nothing wrong with changing your mind if you're not ready."

"Thank you, Jackie," Sarah acknowledges. "But we both know it's time, and I've already spent most of the past week convincing myself that it's the right thing to do. You agree with me, don't you? This is the right thing to do, isn't it?"

She looks to Jackie for encouragement that this course of action will ultimately be for the best, but hoping that her friend will instead convince her that this is all a mistake and that this way of thinking should be abandoned for a more promising and hopeful outcome. As expected, however, her friend is steadfast in her resolve, as she is the one who first initiated the conversation many months ago that has led to this day's decision.

"You know I believe it is the right thing to do," Jackie expresses softly to Sarah. "We all do. But that doesn't mean your feelings shouldn't be taken into consideration, or that whatever it is you decide is secondary to what anybody else, or even me, tries to convince you of. None of us are in your shoes, and none of us could even begin to imagine what this must be like for you. Only you can make that decision, and in the end, only you have to live with that decision. But either way, I will be there for you to help you through it."

Sarah's eyes once again well up with the customary liquid emotion that she has gotten used to over the years. She pulls herself forward into Jackie's embrace once more, squeezing ever more tightly than the last.

"You're right," Sarah whispers as she musters enough control to hold back the tears from escaping. "And this is the right thing to do, and I am ready. I couldn't do this without you, Jackie. I am so glad we became friends."

They relax their hold on one another, and slowly separate. Sarah realizes that she has lost track of time this morning, and her appearance is still in shambles. She has quite a bit to do to make herself more presentable before she can take the ride with her friend.

She immediately apologizes to Jackie, for which Jackie responds that no apologies are necessary. Then Sarah quickly makes her way into the kitchen to put on some coffee.

"Give me just a bit to clean myself up," Sarah explains. "Help yourself to some coffee when it's done and I'll get ready as quickly as I can."

"Don't worry about it," Jackie assures her. "Take whatever time you need."

Sarah nods and makes her way back down the hallway to her bedroom. As she does this, Jackie sits down at the kitchen table waiting for the coffee to finish brewing, but more importantly, she listens keenly to the progress that Sarah is making in her attempts to ready herself. In moments, Jackie hears what she has been waiting for; the shower turns on. With Sarah now fully distracted in her efforts, Jackie can now take this time to do what she furtively came here to do. She stands from the table and makes her way to the room that Sarah refers to as her "special place." In this room, Jackie is sure she will find what she is looking for. For the years that the two of them have been friends, never once has Jackie been allowed into this sacred place. She knows of it only in the heartfelt stories that Sarah would relay to her in her frequent visits. Now, she thinks, is her opportunity to finally set things right.

She enters the room very hesitantly. She knows she has very little time before Sarah is finished with her shower, and she knows, too, that she cannot be caught snooping here without everything being lost. She feels she has worked too long and hard to get to this place to make a careless mistake now. Jackie slips into her thoughts, and for the briefest of moments, the past years come rushing back to her, telling a vivid story of how this moment came to be. She recalls the first time she met Sarah.

It was six years ago. Jackie had just started working in the Severe Trauma Ward just days before a young boy had been rushed into the emergency room with life-threatening injuries. He had been struck by a car, a victim of a hit and run while riding his bike on the street in front of his house. She remembers seeing him being rushed-in that night. Although she was not part of the emergency staff, she was on her break heading to the cafeteria to get a quick bite to eat when the doors burst open just ahead of her revealing first response medical staff wheeling the gurney in carrying the boy. She remembers seeing the significant amount of blood that had soaked into the rolling bed as they passed by her, and the child's hand hanging just over the side having little droplets of blood falling from it forming a faint trail of crimson down the hallway. He spent the rest of that night and most of the next day in surgery. It would not be until two weeks later that Jackie would see the boy again.

As it were, the boy would survive his serious injuries, but not without complications. As a safety mechanism, the boy's brain had all but shut down leaving him in a non-responsive coma. Expected to live, and with his injuries being downgraded over the next two weeks, he was moved from the Intensive Care Unit to the Severe Trauma Ward where Jackie and her staff would take over the patient's care for the remainder of his time in the coma. It was not all that unusual for a victim with severe injuries, such as this boy had, to fall into a temporary coma while the mind and body battled to heal themselves. In Jackie's experience, many such victims would awaken from the coma in one or two weeks; perhaps even a month in more extreme circumstances. But that was not to be the case with this young boy who came into her care that afternoon oh so many years ago. Daniel was his name, and Sarah, his mother.

Jackie's thoughts snap back to the present where she finds herself standing in the young boy's room. She immediately notices how clean it is, and realizes that Sarah probably works so very hard cleaning it even better each time one of her outbreaks takes hold of her and causes her to create such wreckage. Sarah has mentioned it many times to her over the years each time such an incident arose. Jackie scan's the room intently, seeing all the normal signs indicating that a nine-year-old boy once resided within these walls.

There are pictures of his little league team upon the dresser in front of her. Several movie posters hang about the walls behind her. Toy military men are set up along the backside of a desk in the far corner of the room. To the side of her lays his bed made up neatly with superhero coverings and pillowcases. And there, just beside the bed on the nightstand, sits the item for which she dared enter this room. It is the book that each night Sarah uses to comfort her tormented thoughts. It is this very same book that was left in Jackie's care several months ago when Sarah left for Florida.

Sarah had asked Jackie if she wouldn't mind occasionally reading this book to Daniel in her absence, which of course, she agreed to do. But on the first night Jackie sat beside the boy to begin reading, she very quickly realized what this book was, and immediately stopped reading it to Daniel. Of course, she didn't tell Sarah that. As far as Sarah is concerned, Jackie read this book to her son as often as she could. But upon Sarah's return from Florida after receiving the bad news of her son's worsening condition, Sarah had since taken the book back into her custody. And now, with this dark day being realized after so many years, Jackie feels this is the best opportunity to relinquish this book from Sarah since she will no longer need it anymore. She must get rid of it so that no one else can read from it again. She knows she could have gotten rid of it at any time during Sarah's absence. The opportunity certainly was there, but that would have led to too many questions once Sarah returned; questions Jackie couldn't afford being asked of her. No, she thinks, this is a much better opportunity, as now suspicion can't be cast in any one direction, and it will simply look like the book has been misplaced.

So with that in mind, she quickly snatches it from where it rests and heads back out into the kitchen where she shuffles it into her purse that had been left hanging from the chair she had been sitting in. Feeling pleased with herself, she begins to make herself a cup of coffee just as she hears the shower turn off.

She lets out a sigh of relief in the thought that she was able to retrieve the book just in time, and that now all will end as it should.

Moments later, Sarah makes her way into the kitchen draped in a long white robe, a towel still wrapped about her head.

"Jackie," Sarah begins, "I know I've asked you this at least a hundred times in the last few months, and I'm sorry for continually bringing this up, but can you explain to me again what happened the night of Daniel's episode? It's all just... just so... I don't understand it at all."

Sarah sits down heavily across from Jackie and slides her arm across the table toward her. Jackie responds to this motion by grabbing Sarah's hand and squeezes it gently.

"Don't do this to yourself, Sarah," Jackie replies. "It won't change anything about what happened that night, and you'll only make yourself sick."

"I just need to know, Jackie. I just need to hear it one more time before I go through with this. Please!"

Jackie looks across the table into Sarah's swollen eyes. She knows how stubborn Sarah can be, and realizes that she won't let this go until she is once again reminded of what happened to her son that dreadful night. It is, after all, the reason why she is left with making this awful decision that no parent should ever have to make. It is a story that Jackie herself doesn't fully understand. What is it indeed that happened to Daniel? He seemed to be fine one moment, and then the next...? She closes her eyes for a moment to gather her thoughts, takes in a deep breath, and then begins...

"I was working the night that it happened. Sheila, the nurse scheduled on the shift before me, had just left for the evening. You've met her a few times before; she's the one who has dark hair with a white streak in it. Anyway, she, like many of us, normally takes care of rotating Daniel onto his sides and back and massaging his muscles to keep them stimulated and active. She didn't get a chance to do it that night due to an outburst from another patient that took place down the hall. Security had to get involved, it was a messy situation, and she just didn't have the time. So she filled me in on what still needed to be done, and it was no big deal. It was all normal routine.

"I took care of rotating and massaging Daniel like I had done many times before, but then I had to leave the room for a moment to attend to a patient in the next room. When I returned, which couldn't have been more than ten minutes, Daniel was sitting up in his bed, completely motionless, with his eyes wide open staring straight ahead. It took me by surprise. I froze for a moment, not having seen this from any comatose patient before. I could feel my heart pressing against my chest at that moment. I think it was that sudden feeling that brought me back to my wits. I called out for doctor Stevens to come quickly. I ran over to Daniel to check on him. I couldn't believe he was sitting up. He had been in a coma for six years. In my mind, there's no way he should have been able to just sit up like that. It's just not possible. I grabbed hold of both his shoulders to prevent him from falling to either side, and I noticed how cold he was to the touch. He did not feel like that at all just ten minutes earlier while I was working his muscles. Just then, the doctor made his way into the room and asked me to step aside. As soon as I let go of him he started shouting incessantly about his brother dying and about his bicycle."

At that point, Sarah slaps one hand down on the table interrupting Jackie in her story. It is not in anger that she does this, or perhaps it *is* in some manner, but more out of frustration and confusion as to what she is hearing. She has heard the story before, not just from Jackie, but from Dr. Stevens as well, and each time she is perplexed at this same part in the account.

"I don't understand that!" exclaims Sarah. "Daniel never had a brother. Why would he be shouting something like that? It just doesn't make sense to me. It's the first time in six years that he has shown any sign of consciousness, and that's what he…"

She stops in her ranting for a moment, realizing that she is beginning to raise her voice to somewhat of a shout. She drops her face between her palms to gather herself a bit. After a minute of silence, and once she has calmed her emotions, Sarah continues…

"I'm sorry, Jackie. I didn't mean to raise my voice. It's not at you, you know that."

"I know," Jackie replies. "Don't worry about it. I don't have to continue if you don't want."

"No, please go on," Sarah insists. "I need to hear it one last time. Please!"

Jackie nods, and after a brief hesitation, continues from where she left off.

"At that point, still sitting up in his bed, he started yelling out strange words that I couldn't understand. I've never before heard anything like what he was saying. It was all very strange and somewhat frightening. Then he began to flail his arms around in an extremely violent manner while he continued shouting. The doctor asked me to help him restrain your son, but before I could even react to the doctor's order, Daniel began convulsing wildly. And then, almost as quickly as it had begun, it stopped, and Daniel's body suddenly became limp and he slumped backward in his bed motionless once again. I had never seen anything like it. The doctor began to check his vital signs, and I think he knew right away that something was different. Daniel's pupils no longer reacted to stimuli as they had before when the doctor moved his head from side to side, and it seemed that his breathing was becoming increasingly shallower. He had not been on intubation or ventilation since he was first admitted six years earlier, but now it seemed that the need for it was immediate and unavoidable.

"Dr. Stevens ordered a lumbar puncture be given to measure the pressure of the cerebrospinal fluid, and that an EEG be done to check brain electrical activity. He also ordered that Daniel be prepped for a CT scan as soon as the EEG had been recorded. In a few hours, after seeing the results of the EEG and the CT scan, it was all very clear to the doctor. The EEG showed an extreme diminishment of electrical activity registering from Daniel's brain. Even worse, the

CT scan picked up large gray areas throughout the entire cerebrum, the outer region of the brain that controls most all thought processes and motor controls. After several other tests were performed, the doctor concluded that Daniel had fallen into a vegetative state. Although it is still unclear what caused it, what was known for sure was that Daniel would never again wake from this state that he had fallen into. He showed no brain activity, no reaction to outside stimuli, and he now needed to be on a ventilator to keep him alive. He was, for all intents and purposes, brain dead."

"Sarah, I'm so sorry that this happened and that you had to receive that phone call. I wish there was something I could say or do to change all of this. Nobody should have to go through what you are going through right now."

Jackie could see the tears rolling down Sarah's cheeks, and reached up to wipe them. Sarah instantly pulled away, putting up her arms defensively. The reaction startled Jackie, causing her to almost knock over her coffee cup.

"No, don't!" Sarah exclaimed. "It's ok. I think this is all the tears I have left in me for now. I don't think I'll ever understand why it all happened, and maybe I'm not meant to. Maybe everything does happen for a reason and I just have to live with that."

Even as the words leave her lips, Sarah doesn't truly believe them. She still blames herself for being away when her baby boy needed her. Through the last of her tears, Sarah manages to form a half-hearted smile.

"I'll get through this."

She pushes herself back from the table and confidently stands to her feet; perhaps from hearing her own encouraging words.

"Let me just finish getting myself ready," Sarah says as she begins to walk back down the hall. "And then we can go."

As she does so, Jackie reflects on the story she just told Sarah. She knows much of what she said was unquestionably true, and no one could argue any differently. What she could not tell Sarah however, was that the strange words that Daniel had been screaming out; the very words that she claimed she could not understand; were, in fact, all too familiar to her. This is what set her on her path to making sure that the book she placed in her purse moments ago; the book that she took from Daniel's bedroom; the book that Sarah would read from each night; would be destroyed. She knew from that first moment she sat down next to Daniel and tried to read from it that this would eventually need to be done. And it became that much clearer to her when he sat up in his bed that night and began shouting out those words. No, not words, but names. Those names she thought she would never hear spoken from the lips of one such as this child; Ygdarmisalenthinoleptuforniuxym and Mrgreeginthuliuptimonadisanemth.

Chapter 9

Elsewhere

Staring at the image cast before me in the mirror, I can't help but think that this is something that I was probably never meant to see. And yet, here I am gazing at it right before my very eyes. What on Earth could...

"Not Earth, Eddie." The silence is broken as Mr.Greeg interrupts my thoughts, "Not even remotely close."

I turn toward Mr. Greeg, his eyes affixed on the scene splashed on the mirror behind me.

"You... you knew what I was thinking?"

"Of course, Edward," Ygdarmisalenth explains. "Just one of the many talents we have at our disposal. You've already seen and felt a few others. Shall I remind you of some?" Ygdarmisalenth chuckles to himself.

Still very much confused, and admittedly a bit frightened, I turn my attention back to the unholy vision that these two men have opened up before me.

My eyes refocus and pierce deep into the image on the mirrored wall. Like a recurring theme, I once again feel the hair on the back of my neck stand upright followed by a sudden chill that runs the length of my spine. The image shown to me is that of a darkened landscape, similar in appearance as that of a sprawling desert, only this one is bathed in fire and destruction across its rolling hills. Clouds of red and orange smoke billow forth from the ground and swirl about in the wind, making it very difficult to capture all the details through the haze. One detail, however, that has most assuredly not escaped my sight at all; and is, in fact, the sole reason a feeling of utter dread has crept its way into the core of my soul; is the image of so many lifeless bodies that lay strewn across this hellish landscape.

"Nope," Mr. Greeg chimes in. "Not that place either."

With that comment, I realize that my thoughts have once again been violated by the grim figure sitting to my right. I don't feel very good about that at all. I am going to have to try to keep my feelings more closely guarded; if that is even possible.

My gaze still fully concentrated on the wall of images right in front of me, my ears listen intently for any sound of unusual movement behind me. They capture an apparent slight wheezing sound that has returned to Mr. Greeg's heavy breathing. I peripherally see Ygdarmisalenth make his way closer to the mirror; his eyes engaged wholly on the scene being played out before us.

It is an incredulous scene for sure. Bodies of men and women, bloodied, broken, even torn apart in some cases. There is a pathway leading up one of the hills, which is marked by a row of spears that lay host to several impaled bodies. There are a few scattered remnants of concrete buildings about, which I can only imagine based on the magnificent architecture of the structures left standing, were probably quite majestic at one time. Most of them, however, appear to now lay in ruin. What is this I am looking at? Why am I being shown this?

As if in answer to my questions, Ygardmisalenth points forward into the horrific setting, and begins to speak.

"This, Edward, is a place that has been written about many times, inaccurately I must add, throughout the history of your people, even though, until today, it had never once been seen by mortal eyes. Some have called it Purgatory; others call it Limbo; but we, my good friend Mr. Greeg and I, and many others of our kinship, know it as... Elsewhere. Despite the stories, it is not a place where condemned souls go to reside for all eternity trapped between the wondrous light of Heaven above and the fiery pits of Hell below. In actuality, it has been forever forbidden for your kind to ever walk between the barrier of your mortal plane and this one. Elsewhere is a place beyond any human comprehension, where angels of high order are sent to recover after their Earthly assignments have been successfully realized. Not even lower class angels are privileged enough to bask in the glorious wonderment of its surroundings. It is a gateway, a stopping point if you will, to rid ourselves of the rot and stink of the vessels we inhabit. It is a place that allows us to cleanse ourselves of the darkness and impurities of having been among your people, before continuing and passing through into the great brilliance of our sacred home. I only show it to you now so that you may bear witness to the dire situation in which we find ourselves in at this time.

"Elsewhere did not always look like the images being shown to you now on this wall of glass. What you see before you is but a glimpse of what has become of Elsewhere over the past eighty-eight of your human years, and unless we can rectify the unimaginable tragedy that has taken place there, Mr. Greeg and I are stuck here with no means of return. As you can clearly see from Mr. Greeg's outward appearance, and the sudden return of his labored breathing, our vessels are slowly weakening and withering away, and if that should happen while we are here on your plane of existence, then we shall cease to be."

With those words, I can't help but look once again in the direction of Mr. Greeg to confirm what Ygdarmisalenth is saying. It appears he states the truth as, in the brief time I have been sitting here listening to the ramblings of this so-called angel, it seems a darkened lesion has formed on the portly man's left cheek. Mr. Greeg simply shrugs his shoulders as if to pass it off as nothing to be concerned with. I then turn my attention to the man seemingly running the show and wonder why his appearance or health doesn't seem to have the same degradation as that of Mr. Greeg. It only stands to reason that if the-se "vessels" are withering away as he claims, that it would be happening somewhat equally to both men.

As if in response to my unspoken question, Ygdarmisalenth speaks.

"Certainly a reasonable inquiry based on your observation. I mentioned to you about our Earthly assignments, but let me elaborate a bit. We angels, when tasked with an assignment, are sent here in pairs. There is a certain hierarchy among angels that dictate the exact pair to be sent. One angel's purpose is to complete the assignment they are charged with, in full, while the other's sole responsibility is that of the protection of the first at any cost. In my and Mr. Greeg's case, it is I who was honored with this most important of assignments, and it was Mr. Greeg who was charged with my protection; at... any... cost. This vessel I inhabit is still in reasonably good condi-tion because my large friend here has been sharing his light with me, his very life-force if you will, so that I may remain strong enough to carry out my as-signment. In doing so, his vessel has been deteriorat-ing at a much quicker rate than that of my own. In short, he is, as you would call it in your temporary existence, dying. And he will continue to bathe me in his brilliant life essence until his last breath so that I might carry on that much longer to ensure that our mission is put right and on the path to success."

"Wait a minute," I jump in. "This is all a grand story and all, but I still don't know what any of this has to do with me. You tell me these things; things that nobody would possibly think are true; a story of angels, of missions... all ridiculousness. You tell me this man that sits beside me is dying, but that his 'light' is keeping you alive. You show me sleight-of-hand tricks and show me fantastic images through doorways and cast on walls in front of me. None of this makes any sense. You tell me these things and ask me to believe you, but say nothing of why I should or how I am even involved in this charade."

I feel my muscles tighten, and my fists clench in anger. My speech has become much faster as well. I can feel my heartbeat pounding through my chest.

"At this point, I have tolerated both of you long enough. Probably longer than I or anyone should have."

"That's just it, Edward," Ygdarmisalenth speaks out. "There isn't anyone else; just you. Besides me and the good Mr. Greeg, who else have you seen or heard from since you have been here? Think hard and you will come to realize, the answer is quite simple. You have been isolated sir. From the moment we finally found you, we had no choice but to bring you here. We felt it to be the safest action while we tested you to be sure. It was also necessary so that you could not be detected by the other."

I interrupt, "What do you mean 'the other?' This is crazy. Why do I let myself get caught up in this nonsense by asking more questions? You haven't answered with anything so far that would make a reasonable man understand. And I am a reasonable man."

"Why, yes you are, Edward," Ygdarmisalenth states. "Indeed, this is exactly how we expected a reasonable man to react. I am quite sure that, had I had any of your earthly upbringings, I too would be in disbelief if I were in your position. However, that is not the case. And I assure you, the questions you have are being answered in the easiest way possible. We must not deluge you with too much too quickly for fear of you going mad. And now, since the answers you seek have been prolonged long enough, shall I continue?"

"Oh wait!" I hear Mr. Greeg's voice erupt suddenly. "Can I have the honor of explaining this part?"

"If it so pleases our not-so-patient guest. What say you, Edward?" Ygdarmisalenth asks. "Shall Mr. Greeg enchant us with his witty banter?"

I sit back in my chair and fold my arms across my chest as I exhale deeply out of my nose to signify a bit of frustration. I suppose that if I am to learn anything at all, I must once again give them a chance to mutter off some explanations. I know now that you can read my mind Mr. Greeg, so go ahead and enlighten me.

As if on cue, Mr. Greeg responds, "Thank you. Nice choice of words by the way; 'enlighten.'"

"You see, kid," Mr. Greeg continues. "It's like this. You've been missing for quite some time. And now we've found you. And we gotta save you, 'cause that's what's gonna save us. That's our mission. YOU are our mission. Hmmm…," Mr. Greeg ponders for a moment. "All this seemed a bit more exciting in my head, but now that I'm saying it, it's kinda not so, you know, exciting."

A slight smirk comes across my face as I shake my head side to side. What is this guy talking about?

"I'll tell you what I'm talking about. Just give me a second to collect my thoughts," Mr. Greeg continues. He takes a deep, wheezing breath, and then begins again.

"Ok, now listen and try to keep up. We were given a mission some time ago. That mission was to save you. But we couldn't find you. It was like you disappeared. You vanished. We searched for years with no luck. And then, a little while back, something must have happened, 'cause suddenly, for the briefest of moments, we felt your presence. It was fleeting, and then it was gone again, but it brought us to the right vicinity where we were finally able to surmise that it was you that we had been searching for. That's when Darmis over there, oh sorry, I mean Ygdarmisalenth; it slips out sometimes; that's when he decided to test you to be sure it was you before we came out and told you all of… this."

Suddenly, Mr. Greeg breaks out in a fit of coughing as he hunches over and stabilizes himself by pressing on the table in front of him with both hands. As the coughing subsides, and the portly man slowly makes his way to an upright position, I notice the smallest droplets of blood now splashed on the table before him.

"It's all right, Mr. Greeg," Ygdarmisalenth chimes in. "I can continue from here."

My attention turns to this man speaking in the hopes to hear something that even remotely makes sense. He continues…

"Edward, we angels have been completing our tasked missions since the beginning of time. In truth, it is what has kept balance in everything that has been created. However, if you gaze once again at our once glorious land, you will see that it is anything but balanced. What once was magnificent and beautiful has now become decayed and full of pestilence. It is because, over the past eighty-eight years, and all the countless missions that my kinsmen have been sent on, not one has been completed. This has never happened before. And with each failure, and with each pair of angels' inability to return, another pair of my kind ceases to be. We have lost countless numbers, and with each loss, the balance between good and evil shifts that much more in the wrong direction. Elsewhere, which had been untouchable for eons, has now been breached many times by unspeakable demon hordes that have been able to penetrate its weakening barrier. Our forces have been able to push them back, but each time we lose even more. If these attacks continue, and evil was to eventually overcome and envelope Elsewhere, it could begin to strain the barrier that exists between it and the holiest of holy places."

"You mean Heaven?" I jump in, in disbelief.

"Yes, Edward. And if that should happen, then I am afraid all is lost."

Having heard more details about the images flashed before me on the glass wall, I inquire further.

"So you say that you and your people; beings; angels; whatever you are, have been completing missions forever, and then suddenly all that stops eighty-eight years ago. None of you angels have completed a mission since? So, what has changed? What is making these missions so difficult?"

"Ah. At last, you are showing signs of acceptance. And with that, we can share more with you. You will recall that we brought you to this place to shield you from the other. Oh yes, Edward, others are searching for you as well. We believe that the dark forces have figured out the means to destroy Else-where, and have sent out their horde of demons to prevent our missions from succeeding. It is those others that have stunted our success. At each turn, they have hindered us in our actions. We believe that when we first found you in that dark, cold place that you were trapped in, there was another on your trail as well."

"It was a terrible demon to be more precise," Mr. Greeg announces in his guttural fashion.

"That is correct," Ygdarmisalenth continues. "We had no choice but to immediately whisk you away to here now. In this place, the filthy demon cannot find you."

"And why is that?" I ask. "What is this place?"

Ygdarmisalenth glances over at Mr. Greeg for a moment before turning his attention back to me.

"I'm afraid, Edward, that is something that will have to wait for now."

I squint my eyes in disapproval at Ygdarmisalenth, then turn toward Mr. Greeg, who has, for the most part, been relatively quiet these past several minutes, save for the heavy breathing and the wheezing sounds coming from his mouth. In just a brief time, his appearance has once again diminished, and he looks like he is weakening minute by minute. The mark on his face has grown in size and appears to have spread downward toward his neck. This man is in bad shape and needs some serious help.

"Ok, I get it. You're running out of time. But you've found me. Here I am. So do what you say you've come here to do, and save me for crying out loud. Isn't that how it works? You save me and then you get to go home?"

My words come out with hints of sarcasm. I can't believe I am still listening to this. Surely I can take down Mr. Greeg in his weakened condition, and get away from these two easily enough. Yet my curiosity is too strong. For now, I elect to stay to try to surmise what it is that is truly going on here.

"If only it were that simple." Ygdarmisalenth lets out what seems to be a sigh. "No, we are not in a position to be able to save you yet. Not everything that you perceive is exactly as it seems. There is something that you have been missing. You must first understand it all, and in doing so, you will see that it is not us who will be saving you at all, but rather that you will be saving yourself."

The self-professed angel in front of me known as Ygdarmisalenth reaches forward with his right hand, and with his index finger extended, touches me on the forehead. And then…

Chapter 10

Blurred Lines

My eyes open suddenly. How long have I been asleep? I glance to my right at the clock on the nightstand, but my eyes have not adjusted yet, and I can't quite clearly make out the numbers. I hear a rustling coming from upstairs, and the clanging of pans which leads me to believe my mother is making breakfast. I pull the covers aside and sit up in bed, rubbing my eyes voraciously to clear away the previous night's buildup of residue that has formed. Once my eyes are fully functional, I let out a loud yawn as I reach up with both arms fully outstretched toward the ceiling. It feels good. Just then, Mom yells down to me.

"Oh good, you're awake."

It seems strange to me, but I think to myself how great it is to hear her voice. I waste no time. I quickly jump out of bed and race upstairs to the kitchen for the morning greeting. Unfortunately, that greeting doesn't come as I had hoped since once at the top of the stairs, as I enter the kitchen, my mother is not there.

"Mom?" I call out. Nothing returned. I try again, louder, and with a little more emphasis.

"Mom!"

Still, there is nothing but silence. Then, a few seconds later, the silence is interrupted by a knocking at the door. I don't immediately make my way to opening it as I figure that must be what my mother has gone off to do; which explains her absence from the kitchen. But then there is a second round of knocking that catches my attention, and I realize that no one is answering it. I quickly make my way to the door before the person on the other side of it becomes disinterested and walks away, and when I open the door, a beautiful sight stands before me. It's Jasmine. My heart pounds in my chest, and I think I feel my knees slightly give out from underneath me. I can't believe she's here. It seems like it's been forever since I've seen her, but I know I must have met up with her earlier this week. Didn't I?

"Hi, Jasmine." I try to keep cool. "What's up?"

"Hi, Edward," she expresses back, her voice sounding so soft and tender. "Is James ready yet?"

The words came and went so quickly that it took a few seconds to register what was just spoken. I'm not even quite sure I heard it accurately. I was, after all, wrapped up in my thoughts of how beautiful Jasmine looked at this moment, and how surprised I was to see her today. I shrug it off for a moment and ask.

"What was that?" I ask, acting as if I didn't quite catch what she had said, for, in truth, I must not have. But before she could repeat herself, a shuffling noise behind me startles me enough to cause me to jump slightly.

"Hey relax, Eddie, it's just me."

It was James, my brother. But how..?

"Hi, Jasmine," he said as he passed by me. "I'm all set." He then grabbed her hand and leaned forward and kissed her on the cheek. All this must have taken just a few quick seconds, but it was playing before me in what seemed like slow motion. I didn't even have time to mumble any words out before my brother turned back at me.

"Don't forget to let Travis out. Last time you forgot and he had an accident on the floor."

And with those final words, he pulled the door closed, and they were gone.

What just happened? What just happened? When did James get home? I didn't even realize he was able to leave the base. Wait. Focus Edward. Your brother just walked out with your girl. And he kissed her. Brother or not, I'm not gonna let that happen. I run out the door as fast as I can to catch them before they leave, but I'm too late, and they are nowhere in sight. I didn't even hear the car drive off. That was way too fast. I don't know where they were going, so I can't go after them. How could James do that to me? He knows Jasmine and I have been an item for some time now. But what about her? She didn't even so much as show any concern about my feelings. I can't believe this. I start to feel a little nauseous as I turn back toward the front door. What am I going to do? This is awful. That was my brother who just betrayed me. I step back inside as I begin to replay in my mind the events that just took place over the last several moments. I know I just woke up, but I'm not so groggy that I could have mistaken everything that just happened. James just walked out with Jasmine. And also, what was that he said about Travis? How does James even know Travis? He couldn't know Travis. I'm feeling a bit disoriented and my hands begin to shake uncontrollably. Just then, from around the corner, a little scraggly dog comes running up to me and jumps up on my leg with its two front paws. What is this, I think? What is going on?

I bend over to pet the animal. "Hey little guy, where did you come from?" A sudden glance at its collar and I can't help but notice the name inscribed on the tag; "TRAVIS."

I quickly stand up, startling the dog as he runs off behind the corner from where he came from. I don't understand what is going on. Whose dog is that? And that name, Travis; that's just weird. Of all the names it could be, his just happens to be Travis. At least now I know who my brother was talking about. I knew it couldn't have been my buddy Travis; since he… since he… died.

A realization hits me like a ton of bricks. Travis died, but that was when I was in the…

But I'm not in the military. I mean, I was. But that was after James had… I mean after we had found out that James…

I reach for the closest wall to try to steady myself, but it doesn't happen fast enough, and I hit the floor hard.

A few moments pass before I begin to push myself back up off from the floor. I feel so confused, as thoughts swirl around aimlessly in my mind. I try to latch on to some of them that might just make a little bit of sense, but it doesn't work. Nothing seems to make sense right now. Could I have been dreaming about it all; James getting killed overseas, me following in his footsteps and going into the military; Travis getting killed? It all seemed so real. But how could it be if James is here right now? This is unbelievable.

After making my way to my feet a little unsteadily, I call out once again to my mother.

"Mom. Hey Mom!"

And still, she doesn't answer back. Maybe she left? But that was way too fast. She must have gone out to the back yard to get her morning smoke in. It was ironic that she would sometimes go outside to get "fresh air," all the while puffing on her cigarette. I head to the back door to check on her, cautiously watching underfoot, wondering where "Travis" had gone off to. I still don't know what that's about, but my mother should be able to answer all my questions and set me straight.

As I step out onto the back porch, I see no sign of my mother, nor do I smell any sign of a lit cigarette.

Like a broken record, I try once again to get her attention.

"Mom!"

And of course, a lack of a response is all I get in return. With no quick answers coming forth, I turn back to head into the house, and as I do, I notice my bike leaning against the back wall beside the door. It's not so much the bike itself that catches my attention, but the large lettering printed on the frame that does it. It couldn't have been more glaring if it was lit up with blinking neon lights. I reach down and rub my fingers across the word that once again causes me to doubt my thoughts and memories. This is my bike, but the name on it... "Trailblazer." That was the name reserved for our sled. And even that we hadn't seen for years since Troy took it. What is going on here?

If it's even possible, I think I feel my heart beating even faster. If my thoughts were playing tricks on me before, now they have my mind spinning. I step back into the house, and as I do, I immediately get hit with a familiar aroma that my sense of smell has not had the opportunity of enjoying for many years. It's the enticing, sweet smell of fresh-baked apple pie. But not just any apple pie; it was one of Mrs. Kaplan's amazing apple pies. Mom's pies have never smelled quite like this. I turn the corner entering the kitchen, and there it is, sitting ever so deliciously tempting on the counter; a freshly baked apple pie. My mouth begins to water as I see the edges of the pie erupt slightly with gooey succulence from under the perfectly formed golden-brown crust and drip onto the counter.

Now, I like to consider myself somewhat intelligent, and I may not always be the most attentive when it comes to details, but I know that pie was not here a little earlier when I was in the kitchen. Certainly, the smell alone would have alerted me to its presence. But it is most definitely here in front of me now. There's no way James placed it there before coming to the door, and mom is still nowhere around. And it sure as hell wasn't Mrs. Kaplan herself who rose from the dead to tease me with one of her mouth-watering apple pies.

This is getting ridiculous. Am I still asleep, drifting away in my thoughts? The fact that I even think such a thing tells me I am not. Am I going crazy or something? I need to get a grip, but my heart is pounding in my chest, and I feel it getting difficult to breathe. A sudden feeling of fear grips me, but with it, an urgency that gives me an idea.

I run to the phone to call over to Jasmine's house. Maybe she and James were heading back there. Even if they weren't, perhaps her parents know where they were going. If so, and if it's someplace close by, I can at least take my bike to meet up with them.

My shaky fingers race across the buttons with a hurriedness that matches the rhythm of my pulse. I'll get to the bottom of this yet. As I hear the ringing begin, I quickly glance around looking for any signs of our four-legged friend that scuttled off moments ago. I begin to pace around looking for Travis while I await someone on the other end of the line to answer. Then finally, the ringing stops as I hear some shuffling noises come from the other receiver as it is being answered.

"Hello?" comes a soft female voice.

"Hi, Mrs. Gradie," I reply. "This is Edward. Is Jasmine home?"

"I'm sorry, I think you have the wrong number," is what I receive back.

With a slight embarrassment I softly reply "Oh, I'm sorry." and I hang up the phone.

In my haste, not to mention my shaking hands, I must have mistyped the number. I quickly listen for a dial tone once again and then begin dialing Jasmine's number a second time, taking care to pay attention to each button I press. This time, it doesn't take as long for someone to answer the phone.

"Hello?" I hear once again in a familiar tone that sounds very much like the previous woman's voice.

Nevertheless, I reply. "Hello, is Jasmine home?"

And as I had feared, the same response; "I'm sorry, you're calling the wrong number. Who is it you are trying to reach again?"

"I'm looking for Jasmine Gradie."

"I'm sorry child, you've reached the Miller residence. There is no Jasmine here."

When I hear those words, I almost drop the phone. A lump forms in my throat as my mind races to piece together what is going on. I gather my wits and try to clear my throat to speak.

"Um, sorry. You said the Miller residence?"

"Yes I did," she replied in a soft, elderly sounding voice.

At this point, I am almost certain I dialed the correct number this time around, and yet here I am speaking with someone that I shouldn't be talking to. In fact, as if by some weird coincidence, this person just happens to be named Miller, which is the name of the former residents of the house that Jasmine's parents bought. As nervous as I am, I feel compelled to ask.

"This may sound like a silly question," I say with a slight quiver in my voice. "But may I ask, is this the Miller residence at 44 Helms Lane?"

The line is silent for a moment, making me wonder if I had accidentally been cut off. But then…

"Yes, it is," the woman on the other end replies. "Who is this?"

I hear a muffling sound come from the other end which leads me to believe she is trying to cover up the mouthpiece of the phone. She doesn't do a spectacular job with it, as I can still hear her speak, albeit in a muffled fashion.

"Bud, you need to come over here. There is a boy on the phone asking funny questions. He's called twice now."

With that, I immediately hang up the phone. I've heard enough. I feel light-headed, and I feel my mouth has suddenly gone dry. She called out to "Bud." I know I heard that. "Bud." I assume she was calling for her husband, Bud Miller.

Ok Edward, think. Bud Miller, at least the Bud Miller who lived at 44 Helms Lane, was killed when his tractor ran over him one morning when he was working in his field. I know that happened. So how does what I just heard make any sense? I just called over to Jasmine's house, which used to be the Miller's house, and I think I may have just gotten Mrs. Miller, who I couldn't have possibly gotten. And worse, she called out to her dead husband.

The room begins to spin all around me. I feel like I am going to pass out. My stomach begins to churn and my legs weaken as I find myself dropping to the floor on all fours. Once again, my hands begin shaking uncontrollably. My breathing has become very shallow and I begin to dry-heave. It's all I can do to keep the contents of my stomach from coming up into my throat. What is going on? This has to be some kind of joke that someone is playing on me. Why would anyone go to such lengths, and why? This whole morning has been strange. Everything has been twisted. And where is my mother? She could fix all of this madness. Why did she disappear so quickly and not give a reason? I can't believe she would be mixed up in any prank. What happened last night after I went to bed? It was last night, wasn't it?

Am I dead? I don't feel any different physically. It sure would help explain what I am experiencing and why I seem to be communicating with people who, as far as I can remember, are supposed to be dead themselves. I know I'm awake, as I slap myself across the cheek to check if I experience the pain. I do. Would I be able to feel it like that if I were dreaming? I guess I don't know that for sure, but I just know I'm awake right now. Does that mean everything else was just a dream then; before I awoke this morning? Wait, I don't even know if it's morning. I need to pull myself together and get my breathing under control. Calm yourself, Edward. I close my eyes and take in a few deep breaths. Once I feel like my breathing has become a bit steadier, and my hands have slowed their constant trembling, I push myself up from off the floor to check the time. My legs feel like jelly, but I manage to balance myself.

I step through the kitchen entryway to get a clearer look at the clock on the wall, and as I pass by the counter, I stop for a moment and glance back at it. Mrs. Kaplan's apple pie, that moments ago occupied the space on the counter just in front of me, is now gone. But it was there minutes ago. I know it was. I smelled it. I saw it. It was right there, and now it is not. I can't take this anymore. I turn back ahead of me to check the clock, as was my intention in the first place before my attention got diverted to the missing pie. As I look up to the clock above the sink, I once again am reminded that something incredibly strange is happening. The slender hands on the clock are freely spinning in a counter-clockwise motion, and at a very quick pace. Am I on something? Did I take anything last night to help me sleep? I don't remember that at all. I just know that things are not right.

I quickly race back down the basement stairs to my bedroom. I grab my shoes and hastily throw them on as fast as I can. I am going to find out what is going on here. If not from here in my own house, then I will find someone to make sense of this for me. I grab my hat and my jacket and waste no time getting back upstairs to make my way out to…somewhere. Anywhere really, will be better for my sanity than right here. I head to the front door once again, this time for a more focused purpose. As I open it and step out onto the front porch, a sudden calmness embraces me. I reach back to close the door behind me, and as I turn forward once again…

Chapter 11

Worlds Collide

I'm back! But what was that? *Where* was that? It was home, but it wasn't home.

"That is quite right, Edward," the oh-so-familiar voice of Ygdarmisalenth rings out. "Home, but not home indeed."

I thought I was confused before, but now this so-called angel who stands before me has dialed that confusion up a notch.

"You said things would be clearer. You told me I would understand." I begin to raise my voice. My shoulders tense up until I feel a throbbing coming from the back of my neck. "All you've done is to add another layer of confusion. That place wasn't right. Everything was all mixed up. I thought I was dreaming or dead or something. How could I have understood anything from what you just showed me?" I feel my jaw tighten as my teeth grind together in anger.

"That's just the point now isn't it, Edward?" Ygdarmisalenth chimes in. "You can't understand something that isn't real. It's not real. None of it is. Those 'memories' you have, of your life. You can't keep them straight because those memories don't exist."

"What are you talking about?" I yell out. "My memories don't exist? Those are my memories. They are real. You've done something to jumble them up. I don't know how, but you have. You're just sounding stupid now."

"Resorting to derogatory remarks now, are we?" Ygdarmisalenth states this as I notice the expression on his face becomes almost that of disgust, before quickly changing once again back to the stoic, emotionless look that has become a staple of his outward appearance.

He continues… "Don't you see, Edward? These thoughts, these 'memories' you have, they are not real. They are figments of a life that you did not participate in. They have been forced upon you. You see them as real, but they are not, and dare I say, have never been. And until you realize this and accept it as truth, I am afraid we are all stuck here."

I am listening to everything that is being spoken, and I am trying to process it as fast as I can. My brain can only take so much in such a short period. I begin to wonder if the insanity of it all is getting the best of me. After I think I am finally going to start receiving answers that I can understand, instead, all I seem to get is caught up in more convoluted stories that cause chaos to my mind.

"Chaos, kid... (cough, cough), that sounds about right," Mr. Greeg adds, as I am once again reminded that my thoughts are free reign to these... beings.

"You see," Mr. Greeg continues. "It's what (cough) we have had to (cough, cough) deal with for quite some time now. Imagine trying to find something that you know is one thing, but you can't seem to locate it because it has disguised itself as (cough, cough) something else. In case you haven't figured it out kid, that 'something' I am referring to, is you (wheeze)."

"Take it easy, old friend," Ygdarmisalenth says. "You're only wearing yourself down that much quicker."

Ygdarmisalenth then turns his attention back to me. "It's the reason why we couldn't locate you. We were searching for... ahem... someone different, you could say. Someone not quite like you see yourself."

He points a finger in the direction of the mirrored wall to have me look at it, and I am guessing, my reflection.

"Yeah?" I question. "What?"

Ygdarmisalenth lets out a heavy sigh before stating what I had, by now, figured was going to be his next words.

"That's not you, Edward! As much as you see yourself in that very reflection before you and try to believe it... it simply is not you. Try, Edward! As much as we have shown you, as much as you have witnessed and heard, try to look deeper than what your eyes show you now upon that wall."

I hear what the man is saying, and as unbelievable as it sounds, the sincerity in his voice is enough to make me stand there for a few moments and gaze hard at my reflection looking back at me. As silly as it may be, I can't help but think that, to me, I look like me. Isn't that what everyone thinks when they look at themselves. Then there is the thought of me letting myself get caught up in the belief at all; the belief that this man could be telling me the truth.

I take a step closer to the mirror to get a better look at myself. I have aged a bit. There are lines on my face that I don't remember having before. Before what though? As much as my face is familiar to me, it is also somewhat of a stranger to me. I reach forward with my right hand and press my palm against the palm being reflected at me. I then take my forefinger and trace over the lines of the face staring back at me. Each wrinkle, each blemish I keep hoping will help shed some light on what is real and what is not. It is me I am seeing, that much I am sure about. What are these angels trying to get me to see? Why is it all so confusing?

A loud fit of coughing breaks my concentration for a moment as I turn my attention to the ailing Mr. Greeg who is slightly bent over the table trying to regain his composure. Upon him doing so, I once again turn back to my reflection and am quickly startled by what I see. By reflex alone, I jump back about two feet from the glass.

"What is it, Edward? What do you see?" Ygdarmisalenth asks.

"You… you don't see it? You don't see… me?" My lips quiver as the words are spoken. My eyes remain glued to the image cast in front of me.

"Of course we see it, Edward," Ygdarmisalenth continues. "Do you?"

I begin to ask myself that very question. Do I? Do I see what is shown to me? Do I believe it? And yet, I feel a sense that I should. I recognize the familiarity of it. But how can it be? If what I see is me, then it is not me. At least it is not the me that I have known this entire time that I have been here. I look at the glass before me, yet a child stares back. This is not me as a child. I was… I had… what? Think!! My thoughts have suddenly become scrambled and hard to focus on. I know they are there, but they seem a bit foggy right now.

"Don't struggle too hard with this, Edward," Ygdarmisalenth says. "Let yourself overcome what your mind is telling you can't be real, and instead give in to what *is* real."

I close my eyes tightly and grab my head with both hands to try to focus my thoughts. Images flashing in my brain flicker on and off as I try to determine which ones I should latch onto. There is a house. Is it my house? I see a woman making an apple pie. It's not Mrs. Kaplan though. Is it my wife?

Am I married? I can't remember. Then the image is gone as fast as it appeared. Now there is a man that I recognize, but I don't recognize. But that image also is swiftly gone from my mind. I don't understand what is going on here. At once I open my eyes and I am...

"Oh, there you are." Sarah gasps as she struggles to open the oven with her hands full. "Can you help your mom out here and open the oven for me? I'm making your favorite; apple pie."

Daniel gladly does as instructed, since he knows that the sooner the pie goes into the oven, the sooner it will be coming out of the oven ready for consumption.

"Mom, can I go outside and ride my bike? I'll stay on our street," Daniel asks with great enthusiasm. It is a new bike after all. "The Trailblazer!" And he was all too ready to start blazing some new trails with it.

"Yes you can, young sir," Sarah replies. "But only for about a half-hour. Then I want you to come inside to wash up for dinner. And don't forget your helmet and pads."

Already halfway to the door from his mother's initial response, a resounding "I won't" comes from Daniel's lips, as he quickly races out.

He was so excited to finally get a new bike. His last one was a hand-me-down from his Grandparents. They told Daniel it was his father's from when he was a child. That in itself was a great gift to have since he never met his father. He had been killed in the war while Sarah was pregnant. He's heard all the stories from his mom and his Grandparents; about how his father was such a brave man, and an even braver soldier. And the pictures Daniel has of him on his dresser certainly depict a man who looks like he oozes bravery. He was a gentleman too. Sarah would often tell stories of how kindhearted he was to those around him, and how sweet he was to her. So, although Daniel never had the opportunity to meet this wonderful man, he feels he knows him deep inside. And while he means no disrespect by giving up his father's bike, he was quickly outgrowing it and wanted one that he could call his very own. And now he has it.

Often, Daniel would fantasize while riding it that his bike was the fastest in the city. It was only a week old, but in his imaginative young mind, it had already been put to the test by winning all the racing championships there were. He would even think about the crowds that would gather after winning a trophy in his latest victory. How proud his father would be of him as he is lifted onto his father's shoulders and carried through the streets. The thunderous applause would be so loud as he raises the trophy high overhead relishing in his moment of fame.

It was probably because of this daydreaming that Daniel wasn't paying too much attention to the vehicle coming toward him this day. If he had noticed, he would have seen the car well in advance, swerving back and forth from one side of the street to the other. He would have had plenty of time to get off the street and wait for the reckless vehicle to pass by. But unfortunately, this day, Daniel was caught up in his thoughts.

Screeching tires are what first alerts Sarah, followed by what sounds like a loud banging noise. She instantly panics and drops a plate she had been washing, causing it to shatter on the floor. She is immediately struck with fear and can feel her legs begin to shake. An awful feeling mounts in the pit of her stomach as all sorts of thoughts race through her head. Ignoring the broken glass underfoot, Sarah races to the door as quickly as she can. It's always the first thought that goes through a parent's mind when such a noise rings out. A child outside riding a bike, screeching tires, a banging noise. In many instances, the one has nothing to do with the other, and relief is the overwhelming feeling of the parent. But to Sarah's shock and utter fear, that is not the case today. By the time she makes her way screaming over to his bloodied body, his frail frame tangled among the frame of the bicycle, the car that struck him is long gone. Holding Daniel in her arms, she screams incessantly for someone to call an ambulance. This would be the beginning of the nightmare that is Sarah's world as she knows it.

I snap back to the here and now. The fog is starting to lift and details are becoming clearer.

"Did you see it, Eddie?" Mr. Greeg blurts out. "Did you see what you (cough, cough) needed to see?"

"I saw something," I reply. "I'm not exactly sure what it was yet. Those people… they seemed familiar. I know them, don't I?"

Mr. Greeg tries to speak, but Ygdarmisalenth raises a hand that quickly shuts down a response.

"He must see it for himself, Mr. Greeg; if he is to finally understand. I am sorry, Edward, but you are not quite finished with your enlightenment. I'm afraid you will have to visit those thoughts again. And since we are pressed for time, I will have to speed things up a bit by giving you a little 'push.' Off you go now."

Ygdarmisalenth raises a finger to my forehead, and just as I feel his touch…

Darkness is all that Daniel senses. It envelops him. He thinks he hears noises, voices, but it just sounds like so much gibberish. It's very faint. He wants to scream out, but each time he tries, silence is the only sound he can muster. He feels movement. He feels the subtle hint of touch. He feels pain. For some reason though, it is not the same as what he recalls it should all feel like. Something is different. He doesn't know where he is, or how he got here. He does know he wants his mother. How long has he been without her? Why isn't she here? He thought he heard her for a moment. She was reading to him. It was his favorite book. But then she stopped. Why did she stop? How long ago was that? Why is it still dark?

These thoughts continue to race through Daniel's head. Over and over they come and go. Why did this happen? Where am I? What's going on? Who is that? What did you say? I can't hear you. Why is it still dark? It's so dark. Why won't you answer me? Answer me I said! ANSWER ME!!

At that moment, there is light. Daniel suddenly sits up in the bed that has become his home for the better part of his life, and begins to shout out loud.

"Ygdarmisalenthinoleptuforniuxym!"
"Mrgreeginthuliuptimonadisanemth!"
"Ygdarmisalenthinoleptuforniuxym!"
"Mrgreeginthuliuptimonadisanemth!"

"I am here. Save me. Help! I am here."

"Ygdarmisalenthinoleptuforniuxym!"
"Mrgreeginthuliuptimonadisanemth!"

And then there is silence, and he finds himself back in the dark.

"Wake up, Edward," are the next words I hear. Looking up at Ygdarmisalenth, I realize I must have passed out. That and the fact that I'm lying on the floor is another good indication. The good doctor and his stout cohort help me to my feet. I'm still a bit shaken up from what I just experienced, but it all rushed back to me in a flood of memories and experiences like I had never known. I know how I got here. I know now where I am. I know now *who* I am. And I know these two gentlemen before me. Another world has been revealed to me; a world that just came smashing into the one I am currently residing in. And as these two worlds collide, a surge of energy pierces into me. My blood begins to boil with an outward rage that takes hold of my very being. With the revelation that has now been exposed to me, I know what I must do.

I turn my attention to Ygdarmisalenth, and with a much more confident demeanor, ask a simple request.

"Tell me about this 'Other' you mentioned."

With a subtle smirk as an acknowledgment, Ygdarmisalenth speaks.

"I thought you'd never ask... Daniel."

Chapter 12

Breach

It's all they've known. It is the sole purpose of their being. To share their light and guidance to the wretched souls that reside on the lower plane of existence that has been continually darkened through the ages. They peer into the poor shadows. They watch over the decrepit lives in that other world that is so far removed from their glorious expanse. They see the rot and decay that mortal vessels leave behind them without so much as a care in the world. The dark stink of filth that permeates the physical world is almost unbearable to their kind. But it is why they exist. It is why they have always existed. They serve a higher power. Theirs is a higher purpose that the lives they ultimately affect couldn't possibly fathom. It is beyond mortal comprehension. But still, they perform their tasks as they are appointed. Two by two they go to that place carrying out their carefully instructed plans. Each new mission contrived to bring a slight glimmer of hope and light to the awful exist- ence of what mankind calls lives. A life saved here. A life saved there. A life saved that will eventually spawn a new idea, a new purpose, which will in turn affect, or maybe even infect, many more lives around them in a positive way. This is the way the light can be cast like a blanket over the world of men. Slowly the shadows and the darkness give way to the bril- liance that these other beings altruistically provide. Selfless as they may seem, however, in truth they do these things for purely selfish reasons. They carry out their appointed tasks so that they, themselves, may continue to exist.

It may seem like they serve the unwitting, un- knowing, unacknowledged, unforgiving lives on that earthly plane, but truly they serve only one. And it is a service that is unquestioning and unwavering, for, in return, they are rewarded most handsomely. That reward being allowed to spend their days in this ever wondrous place between planes. This is Elsewhere. And it is a most glorious place.

Another two angels return after having saved a young boy from a burning building in Damascus, Syria. Years from now, this boy will become a surgeon who will save a young pregnant woman that will have been shot several times by a group of Sunnis when she is caught in the crossfire at a religious gathering. She will later give birth to a baby girl who will eventually grow up to discover the cure for a rare disease found in infants that negatively impacts their muscle growth.

Another successful mission completed, they must now rid themselves of their human vessels and cleanse their light of the impurities they have sustained while living amongst people. Only after shedding the filth and depravity of their mortal coil are they allowed to pass through to Elsewhere. Once through to their beloved realm, they are free to enjoy that which is their sole reason for being. And another life saved only helps to strengthen the delicate strand that separates the dark from penetrating the light.

This latest mission was a good win for the angels; since the last pair appointed failed to accomplish what they were sent out to do. It was the first time such a thing had happened, and in failing to complete their task, they perished amongst the human waste, unable to return to their home.

But this pair has indeed made it back unscathed, and can now pass through to their exquisite realm. But upon entering this day, it is immediately noticeable that something is not quite the same. The landscape is unchanged, with the sleek lines of the towers cascading over the hills in the distance. Still present is the clear, unmistakable view that carries on infinitely in all directions. The presence of all the other angels that are their brothers is still a great comfort to them after having been away for a time. But it is the feel of this place that has changed. When they passed through, they did not feel the same soothing warmth that they remembered being so accustomed to. It wasn't cold by any means, but something had been diminished enough to take notice of. They wondered if they were the only ones that noticed this change. Had they been so corrupted during their time away that they can no longer fully experience the wonderment that is their eternal right? Surely in time, they think, things will return to normal for them.

Unfortunately, once a course is set on a certain path, it is difficult to change from that course. In this case, the previous pair of angels had failed to save a man in China from embarking on a dangerous fishing trip. This was a trip he would not return from. He was never meant to go. Instead, he was supposed to have been present at his place of employment on the day an explosion took the life of a co-worker. Had he been at work that day, he would have saved the co-worker from the devastating accident. The co-worker would then later have saved his own younger sister from being brutally murdered during a home invasion. The sister would have gone on to be a leading activist and proponent in helping to limit fossil fuel consumption, thereby leading to less air pollution. But this will never happen. And it was not solely due to mistakes made by the pair of angels. Something else was at play there. Something had found a way to cause the misstep by the pair. And that something wasn't ready to let go just yet.

Soon after, it had been learned that, yet again, another pair of servants had not accomplished their task, and therefore never returned to Elsewhere. Stories of a third failed mission soon spread throughout Elsewhere, and then a fourth. With each failure, the ramifications were felt all over the landscape. Mild changes took hold at first. Some were barely noticeable. But each small change would have a much greater effect on the whole than what was easily seen or felt. Two more angels would be sent out, two more would meet their demise. Every angel in Elsewhere began feeling a sense of uneasiness. They all had but one duty to fulfill, and that duty, however self-sacrificing it may be, is to ultimately protect the greater kingdom beyond. The balance between light and dark is a fragile thing indeed, but it had always been kept in check by the success of their missions. Now that some of those missions had been compromised, and angels were not returning to their home, darkness was beginning to have a tighter grasp than it had ever had before. And the trend would continue for many years to come.

Mission after mission, failure after failure, had cast a feeling of despair over the once magnificent land of Elsewhere. The angels could sense the boundaries of their place of warmth and light weakening, giving way to the ever-strengthening dark. They would continue on their righteous path, setting out to save what lives they were charged with saving, in hopes that they would find success and begin the process of balancing the scales once again. But each new mission was met with failure time and again. And on the forty-third year since the first pair of angels failed to rescue the Chinese man from being lost at sea, a tear in the fabric of their once marvelous landscape began to appear. It was only a matter of time before that tear would become a gaping hole in which the dark forces would be able to penetrate.

The forces of light had always far outnumbered the forces of darkness. Never before would any servant of the dark even try to breach the boundary of Elsewhere. Because of the strength in their numbers alone, and the sheer brilliance that each angel exudes individually; when put together in full force, it would completely decimate any child of the dark in an instant. That had always been their protection. And the lives they save help keep their light strong. But the years have not been so kind. Because of the numerous failed missions, their numbers have decreased significantly, and the strength of their light has faded over time. The uneasy feeling among the angels spreads like a pestilence across all of Elsewhere. And the forces of darkness have grown stronger because of it. Were they strong enough perhaps, to try a siege on this magnificent of places?

They did not have to wait long to find out. The spawns of evil were becoming braver. The first lowly demon broke through the barrier only moments after the initial tear was formed. It was dispelled almost instantaneously. It had been destroyed before any noticeable damage could be done. A single demon is insignificant, but it was still a great concern to the angels. Nothing like this had happened before, and it was uncertain what this latest act would invite. And where there is one, others would surely follow. The destruction of a single malevolent creature forces the angels to expel a small amount of their light force. They would have no problem holding back dozens of these wicked annoyances; but what about hundreds or thousands? How long would it be before the demons attempted to start an all-out war with the angels? How long could the angels' light hold the dark beings at bay? This concern caused the angels to start dividing their numbers. There would be those that would go on missions to try to increase the strength of their light, and there would be others that would stay to guard the ever-increasing orifice that had formed in their reality. At this point, the numbers of those in the light still far exceeded the numbers of those in the dark. Although their light had dimmed, together it was still quite strong enough to eradicate any dark threat that would pierce the veil into their home.

Soon enough, a second demon broke through, and again, was immediately exterminated. Time and again, a stray demon would force its way through the breach, only to be dispatched with such swiftness. But these were just low-level demons that posed no real threat at all. They had no real chance against the might of the angels; even angels that were diminished in capacity. But with more and more angels leaving to go on their directed missions and not returning, the ranks of the angels continued to lessen. Their light, too, was fading over time from each failed attempt. And with each demon that would break through the barrier, more of the angels' light was being used up in defense of their sacred realm. The forces of light were slowly weakening, and the real threat had yet to show itself.

Chapter 13

Collapse

She stands over just another tattered body of the many that have once stood in her way. Her lust for death and destruction shows no bounds. She is a true leader, a demon of the highest order; a Dark Queen. The rest of her demon horde make quick work of the dissipating ranks of the angels left behind to protect the gaping rift into this realm. She will let nothing stand in her way. The rubble at her feet is an indication of how easily the great walls and buildings of this once brightly shining landscape have tumbled down about her. She cares not for this place or its inhabitants. They are just pitiful ants, blindly doing their master's bidding; insects that are to be stamped out under her heel. No, she has other plans in mind than just the inevitable destruction of this wretched setting. Hers is a much higher purpose than just to breach the outer haven of Elsewhere. She is focused on causing the complete and utter collapse of what lies beyond this landscape. This day, she has set her sights on the great kingdom itself.

Indeed, her confidence has undeniably been bolstered these past many years, as the proof of her making it this far can account for. She has waited a very long time for this moment. Never previously has her demon brethren even been able to so much as scratch the barrier of light that protects the outer sanctuary surrounding the great kingdom beyond. Now it seems that she has not only scratched and clawed her way into Elsewhere but that it, too, shall succumb to her ever darkening will; much like is happening to the world of man that she has slowly been able to infect over time.

Here, it is not enough for her to simply triumph over her hated rivals of light and righteousness. To destroy them and extinguish their light is but her first evil act. She must leave behind a message to all who dare try to stand in her way that she will not be denied. She instructs her demon horde to continue forward against the weakening angels. She knows her pets, even now, stand little chance of reaching their destination. The angels, though weaker now than they have ever been before in their existence, are still more powerful than her soldiers of darkness. But she knows, too, that with each continued assault, the angels use up more of their essence. With each lowly demon dispatched by an angel's light, the weaker that angel becomes. By the time she reaches that angel, he is barely a threat to her savagery. The darkness permeating outward from her very being grasps hold of the weakened harbinger of light and quenches the last remnants of his radiance. Once snuffed out, to show her defiance of this miserable land and these abhorrent protectors, she tears the lifeless being apart. As a sign of victory, as much as a personal trophy, she impales what's left of the dismantled body on her spear of darkness. She looks around with a boastful gaze at her accomplishments. Many such spears, displaying tattered, impaled angels are scattered throughout Elsewhere. This has become her signature, foreshadowing what her future reign will look like.

She trudges forward, severed limbs and broken bodies under her feet become like a pathway leading her onward. Stepping on the ragged carcasses beneath her is just another example of her disdain for these lighted warriors. She feels no remorse in her actions. Instead, it brings her great pleasure to wreak such havoc to her hated enemies. Angels, be damned, she will stay her course until the light in this land is no more.

The angels' resolve, however, is not so easily thwarted, as they have noticed the need to gather themselves together to work as a cohesive unit. The combined light energy of numerous angels is much more powerful than those of a few. The angels realize this and focus their radiance into a concentrated effort to dispel their common enemies. Even more of their ranks fall-in to add to the intensity of their brilliance. They stand as one; a powerful union of guardians. A swath of light is forcefully expelled from their combined might and pierces through a large contingent of low-level demons. The ground on which they stand rumbles in ferocity. The buildings that once stood as a glorious symbol of their magnificence, tumble before them as they expand their unequaled aura of light far greater than they have ever had to do before.

The angels know what failing to protect this land and that of the great kingdom beyond would mean. If darkness should prevail, it would be the end of everything good and decent. Morality and virtue would disappear from existence. The world of man would dry up and decay. No more light would shine forth leading the way to salvation. Those angels unfortunate enough to be spared would become slaves to the Dark Queen's twisted whims, forced to feed into her darkness. They would be forever beaten and tortured by her and her faithful underlings, merely to show the complete dominance she holds over them. Chaos would rule for all eternity.

Failure, therefore, is not an option. One after another, the angels dispose of demon after demon, making their way forward to increase the span between them and the beloved kingdom they have sworn to protect. The demons that aren't able to avoid the angels' counter are immediately destroyed in an instant from the strength of the luminosity. Every so often, a stray demon penetrates through their protective shield of light and manages to take the life essence away from one of the angels, before being eradicated itself by one of the many who remain undaunted. The angels traverse onward across the landscape, embroiled in this battle between light and dark, dispensing of each member of the dark order swiftly and without mercy, driving forward toward the one who has brought this heavy blight and destruction upon them. She must be ousted if they are to claim victory.

Along the outskirts of Elsewhere, the Dark Queen and her minions of servitude continue to wreak havoc on the singular angels that are intermittently strewn before them. The battle that is taking place this far abroad from the greater kingdom beyond is heavily in favor of the dark army. The number of demons breaking through the gaping rift is a greater amount than what the angels can withstand. As one demon is obliterated by a defending angel, three more pounce upon the weakened guardian of the light. The demons do not know of the pending force that lies ahead of them, but it is only a matter of time before the path they are on brings them in direct conflict with the last bastion of hope for this land.

As small battles rage on, the smell of death engulfs the Dark Queen, fueling her desire to continue forth. Charred bodies of those who once drove her and her dark brothers away are now laden across this vast region. She steps over their shredded bodies as if they are nothing to her. She glances back in delight to witness what she and her evil horde have left behind them. The carnage and devastation that has been left in their wake would surely shake a mortal soul down to its very core. Broken bodies all around, torn limb from limb, cover every part of this land that was once considered beautiful beyond belief. A trail of limp, impaled sentinels that were once proud guardians of this wondrous reality, now forms a roadmap back to the entrance from where Elsewhere was first breached. She embraces the twisted smile that she feels encroach upon her visage. She can't help but think how she has surpassed her brothers in this ages-long quest to conquer the one realm above all others. She also knows she is but the first of the higher order of demons to break through into this land. Should she falter, others will ascend to carry on in her stead. But having been the first, she has no intention of failing.

She turns her attention forward once again, a bead of saliva forming on her lips in anticipation of what is to come. She licks it away in sheer excitement; her gaze fully focused on what lies ahead of her. In the far-off distance, a glow begins to appear. She understands this to mean that her fight has only just begun. The demon horde that had been dispatched ahead of her seems to have raised the ire of this realm's inhabitants. She raises an arm to gather the attention of her malevolent dark forces. Then, with a confident smirk on her face, she points a long misshapen finger toward the glowing light in the distance, signifying that that is the direction where destiny awaits them.

They smash through the remaining tired and withered angels in these outlands at a feverish pace. Their destination has been shown to them in an ever brightening luminescence on the horizon of this deteriorating landscape. Along the way, crumbled walls and buildings, devastating fires, and tattered, lifeless bodies indicate that her lowly pets have done their jobs well.

The angels, too, have done their part in the defense of their home. Ashes floating aimlessly throughout the landscape signify the efforts put forth in defending this land. The light they emit is so powerful that lesser, insignificant demons burst into blood red flames when bathed in it. With their numbers depleted to such a degree, and their light essence dimmed through the years, they have been forced to combine their might in this last hour of desperation. By doing so, they have increased their powerful rays of light to such a degree that no evil force shall stand against them.

When the two factions finally meet, it is almost one-sided. Many of the demons of the dark army are instantly obliterated in the onslaught of the angels' full attack. Those that are not immediately engulfed in flames are blinded by the intensity of the glow that the angels are permeating from their collective beings. Their light is shining so brightly that it scars the foundation beneath them where they travel. The Dark Queen has underestimated how powerful the angels can be when they compose themselves to such a degree, yet she presses on. More of her demon squads continue to bombard the angels with their fierce attacks, but they are unsuccessfully met with death. She knows that the longer her forces can keep this up, the weaker the angels' light will become. In time, it is undeniable; she will overcome the forces of light and finally reach the hall of the great kingdom that has ever been her overreaching goal.

She charges forward, stepping straight into the path of the brilliant glow emanating from the core of the mass of angels. The light, although intense, does not have the same effect on her as it does her lowly brethren. She is not some pitiful demon to be trifled with. It *does* burn her for sure, but she can withstand its shining might longer than those she had sent in previously to perish before her.

Although she is a powerful demon, a Dark Queen, she has overstepped her bounds in this instance. Even her resilience to the radiance of the angels' offense can only withstand so much before the realization takes hold. They are too powerful still. This will not be her day. She must retreat through the gaping maw from whence she came, otherwise all will be lost. If she meets her demise this day, all that she has accomplished will have been for naught. For although her brothers would now stand a better chance against their hated rivals of this Elsewhere, and reaching the great kingdom's sacred dominion, she does not wish to give them the satisfaction of conquering this place after having been the one to finally enter into this domain. She will be the one to eventually extinguish all the light from humanity and shroud the world in darkness.

In a final act of defiance, she lunges forward and snatches the nearest angel that is within her reach. Her fingernails like talons, they rip into the flesh of this herald of light. The pain she feels from the light being bathed upon her is almost unbearable, but she will not let it show. She must let her enemies know that she has won a small victory this day. With the angel still in her grasp, she stares deep into his eyes and lets out a deafening snarl. Then without a moment's notice, the Dark Queen opens her salivating maw revealing a full jaw of razor-sharp fangs, and bites deep into the angel's cheek. Her pointed teeth penetrate through cartilage and bone. The angel's body goes limp in her vice-like jaw. She knows this is not enough. She must make a statement to all those witnessing her vile act. With a contemptible growl, she shrugs her head to the side with such ferocity that it rips the angel's head clean from his body. As his body falls lifeless at her feet, she stands unwavering before the unity of angels. Her dark flesh searing from the incredible light that is assaulting her, she knows she cannot withstand much more. She spits the angel's remains from her mouth and signals for her pets to retreat.

She quickly withdraws her attack and rushes back to the entrance. She knows the angels will not follow her beyond that barrier. At the breach, she turns one last time to gloat about what she has accomplished. Her forked tongue licks away the last of the rotten taste of the angel from her lips before she hurls herself toward the fissure. And then she is through it.

The last of the remaining demon hoard are quickly vanquished by the powerful light emanating from the brigade of angels. While still focusing their combined strengths, they use the extreme heat they are generating to cauterize the crack in the fabric of their now devastated realm. They know they have been weakened this day. They must find a way to regain their strength, for they know another attack is imminent. The Dark Queen's insatiable lust for power and dominance will not be denied, especially after causing such carnage and devastation to their once beautiful Elsewhere. But for now, they are safe for the briefest of moments.

Chapter 14

Escape

Ok, so now I know what I am dealing with. The real question is what do I do about it? How do I... how does anybody... deal with something like this? These angels that stand by my side have guided me this far. They have awakened the memories within me. They have shown me my true self. I am Daniel. I am that young boy lying in that hospital bed. I've known nothing of my life for... how long has it been?

Without letting my attention stray from the image in the mirror, I ask. "How long?"

"It's been six years, kid," Mr. Greeg chimes in.

I turn in shock. "Six years? Six years? I've been lying in that bed for six years? How can that be? I've missed so much of my life!"

I feel like breaking down in a fit of tears but I know I must keep my composure. I have to be strong now. I turn back to the image of my feeble form. Weak, silent, still. I am broken and helpless there. Yet somehow, I am here too. But where is here?

"That is a very good question, Daniel," Ygdarmisalenth interjects. "Where indeed? Although I'm surprised you haven't already surmised the answer yourself."

My thoughts having been pierced once again, I turn to face the angel.

Ygdarmisalenth continues, "Having just fully realized the gravity of the situation you are in, I can understand the confusion. And since we find ourselves in the very same situation as you, I think you can appreciate the haste in which Mr. Greeg and I must ask you to embrace what it is you already know."

"I think what he's telling you, kid," Mr. Greeg adds, "is that we ain't got a whole lot of time left. You do know where you are, don't you?"

"I'm… I'm in… This is my mind."

No sooner do the words escape my lips, than I glean a spark flash from Mr. Greeg's eye. My thoughts in a swirl, I look toward the mirror once again, which before me now confirms all that has been revealed to me. I see the young boy…me, lying in a hospital bed, all but lifeless. Machines humming and beeping, doing what they can to keep me alive. I watch as each expansion of my chest is timed with the expulsion of Oxygen from the nearby ventilator. It is a surreal feeling seeing myself in that bed, yet knowing I have somehow instead been imprisoned in the recesses of my young psyche. I can only presume this was some type of protection mechanism that my brain inflicted upon itself. And now, because of it, I am trapped in here with no knowledge of how to escape. I continue to observe the situation reflected at me when I notice a nurse enter the hospital room with another woman. The woman sits beside the bed and begins sobbing. I reach forward to touch the mirror, my finger tracing the lines of the woman's face.

"Mom!"

I feel a tear roll down my cheek, but then I quickly wipe it away with my other hand.

"That's my mother," I scream out. "What's wrong with her? Why is she crying?"

Ygdarmisalenth peers at me sullenly as he begins to speak. "You are quite right, Daniel, that woman is your mother. She goes to visit your bedside quite often in fact. The crying, too, also takes place quite often. Today she has gone there to your side for a very different reason, however. She intends to let you go."

"What do you mean, 'let me go?'"

"I'm sorry to tell you this Daniel, but today is the day she is saying goodbye to you for the last time. She has gone to the hospital to put an end to your misery, and in doing so, she is hoping it will be putting an end to hers as well."

"She's killing me, you mean," I snap back.

"That's harsh kid," Mr. Greeg chimes in. "But yeah."

"Why would she do this?" I begin to weep. My legs give out from beneath me and I hit the floor hard. I don't feel it. My head is still firmly pressed against the glass as my vision begins to blur from the liquid. The tears continue to flow from my eyes faster than I can wipe them away. "Why would she kill me? What did I do that was so wrong? I didn't mean it. Does she not love me anymore?"

"On the contrary, Daniel, she loves you more than you know."

Ygdarmisalenth's words, although gently spoken, fail to put my thoughts at ease. He continues...

"You must understand Daniel; she has been in agony for the past six years. She has always held out hope that you would one day return to her. She never once gave in to the thought that you would stay in the coma you sustained. But that was before."

"Before?" I question.

"Yes," Ygdarmisalenth replies. "Before the other one had come for you. You know of her now; that evil demon queen who will stop at nothing than to bring damnation upon the great kingdom. She found you, Daniel; in that hospital; before we did. She knows it is our mission to make sure you survive. Look closely, Daniel, at the nurse who stands by your mother's side. She is known to your mother as Jackie, but she hides her true self. It is she who has influenced your mother into making this dreadful decision. It is she who looks forward to your demise. It is she who intends for our mission to fail. And it is she who has unwittingly allowed for us to reach you."

Through my sobbing, I listen intently to what this angel has stated to me. "What do you mean she has allowed you to reach me?"

Before Ygdarmisalenth can continue, an ungodly coughing sound comes from the direction of Mr.

Greeg. Our attention diverts in time to witness him collapse to the floor. He looks to be in awful condition. Not knowing what to do, I can only sit and watch as Ygdarmisalenth rushes to Mr. Greeg's aid. He leans forward and whispers something into the ailing angel's ear, and then presses a hand to his forehead. I stare in amazement as I observe Ygdarmisalenth's hand glow with such intensity that I have to avert my eyes. Then as fast as it began, it has ended. I squint back to Mr. Greeg, my eyes still seeing black spots dancing around. But I also see Mr. Greeg brace himself upon the floor and push himself erect. What just happened? What did I just witness?

"It's simple really," Ygdarmisalenth explains. "My friend needed my help. He has been feeding me his life force all the time we have been here. I could do no less for him in his time of need. That should keep him going for a while longer."

"You shouldn't have done that," Mr. Greeg speaks up. "All you've done is taken away some of your light and weakened yourself."

"Hush, my cantankerous old friend, we'll get through this together. Now, as I was saying, that sinister demon queen made a mistake, and she is the reason why Mr. Greeg and I were able to locate you. She was left in charge of your care for a short time. Your mother had asked this 'Jackie' to read to you from a book. You may know of the book in which I speak."

I do know the book. It is my favorite. My mother would read it to me most nights. It always made me feel safe and comfortable. Even when I was in a horrible mood or feeling sick, that book would always take away my bad feelings. It always reminded me of... of...

I nod in acknowledgment.

"Yes, well, she refused to read that book to you. In doing so, something inside your subconscious must have been building up feverishly until, eventually, it came exploding outward in the form of you calling out to us. At that moment, you pulled us in your direction. It was a start. While you were in that momentary lucid state, you also must have sensed an evil presence around you, and before the dark demon could fully gain control of what little amount of subdued consciousness you had left, you retracted to a 'safer' place. But in doing so, we almost lost you. And I fear you may have doomed yourself in the process. But, there is a way to stop it."

I hear those words and immediately perk up, wiping the tears and snot away from my face.

"Yes," I reply. "Tell me what I have to do. I'll do anything. I just want to be back with my mom."

"Come now, Daniel, I told you what you must do when we first met. You need to 'save us.' But to do that, you must regain control of your psyche. You must get back to your body and awaken from your long slumber. In doing so, you will be reunited with your mother, we will have accomplished our mission and be able to return to Elsewhere, and you will have helped fortify our stronghold from outside influences."

"And how do I do that?" I cry out. "I've been stuck in here with you and haven't been able to figure out where to go. Why can't you just tell me? I can't do it alone. I want my mom. Tell me. Where do I go?"

"My dear boy," Ygdarmisalenth says in a soothing tone, "only you can figure that out. You have been inside your confused head this entire time. Surely you must know the way out. If not, then I fear the worst. Already I can tell that your mind is starting to regress. There isn't much time before your thoughts are too simple to comprehend what we are telling you."

I know what Ygdarmisalenth states is probably true. I can feel it also. My thoughts are becoming hazy. Try to concentrate Daniel. Think! If I put myself in here, then I must know the way out. And it sounds like there is a lot more at stake than just me. But where do I even begin? I twist my head from side to side to re-familiarize myself with my surroundings. There is the mirrored wall behind me. Positioned in front of me are the table and three chairs. To the left and right of me is nothing for as far as I can see. It seems my only way out of here is once again through this mirrored wall. Slowly, I push myself up from off the floor, using the mirror to brace myself up against. I reach for the closest chair and clench it tightly within my hands. Before I can act on my thoughts, I hear Ygdarmisalenth clear his throat.

"Ahem! Daniel, might you consider using the door this time?"

He points behind him to the back of the room, and much like before, a door now stands where it hadn't moments ago. After everything I have experienced, I still find myself shocked with disbelief. I relax my hold on the chair and begin to make my way toward the door. As I do, Mr. Greeg once again breaks down into a coughing fit. I see Ygdarmisalenth attempt to come to the large angel's aid, only to be pushed backward by the stubborn man.

"I can't let you do it again," Mr. Greeg insists. "You are the one that must remain."

With the doorknob in my hand, I look to Ygdarmisalenth, perhaps for some sign of approval.

His sole comment; "Hurry boy, there isn't much time."

That's approval enough for me. I gaze beyond the two angels at the mirrored wall once more to see my mother still crying and holding my hand. "Mom, I love you. Wait for me. I'm coming back to you." Then I glance back to Ygdarmisalenth as if to say 'Goodbye.' And with that final thought, I am out the door.

It has been a while since it has been just me. I am alone once again, like when I first started this journey. I think back and I find it amusing that my goal then was the same as it is now; to escape this place. Only now, my escape has more purpose. I'm trapped in my mind, deep in my subconscious, and I need to break free to recapture my life. It's all very incredible to me, yet somehow strangely makes sense. So here I am back in the hallways. This ever-winding labyrinth that seemingly led me to nowhere hasn't changed at all. The blank walls all around me have no recognizable features on them. The lefts, the rights; they are all the same as before. If this is my mind, what the hell am I thinking? That's just it; I don't know what I am thinking. My thoughts are becoming increasingly confusing to me. I dash down the hallway as quickly as I can, knowing that time is of the essence. I find myself able to move much quicker now that my 'injuries' are no longer a hindrance. I also don't have the fear of the unknown holding me back anymore. My movements don't have to be as cautious.

I come to the end of this passageway, and I am forced to make a choice. I can go left, or I can go right. This place is truly a maze. Is there a right answer? If I choose one way over the other, and it's the wrong way, will I have damned myself and the two angels I left back in that room? Maybe all paths lead to the same place. There *is* such a thing as overthinking. That's what I am doing right now. My mind is racing. I should just pick a direction and stick to it. I look in both directions for an answer, but nothing comes. I find myself frozen; not from fear, but rather from disappointment.

My thoughts wander to my mother as she sits by my bedside crying. I think of Ygdarmisalenth's words about how she has supported me through all the years I have missed, and how I am going to let her down if I don't get out of this hell. I don't want to die. I need to wake up. I need my mom. Why can't I find my way out? I want to get out of here. I want to go home. Why is it so hard to figure out? I just want to make my mom happy. I want to show her I love her and that I didn't leave her. I need to find my way. I promise if I do, I won't leave her again. I won't ride my bike or play in the street anymore. I promise I'll be more careful. I just need to go home and be with you, mommy. I promise I'll be good. I must awaken. Damn you, Daniel, why does your mind have to be so confusing. Filled with frustration, I yell out loud.

"Which way do I go!!? TELL ME!!"

Suddenly the lights go out and I am left in darkness. Then, before my eyes, a light shines down the left corridor. I think I just hit a chord inside this dumb brain of mine. Whatever it is, I'll take the hint. I rush down the left hallway as fast as I can, a single light leading the way. As I reach more entrances, the light continues to indicate which direction I am to follow. I feel a sense of hope come over me. My heart is racing. I am feeling excited for the first time since I have been here. I follow the next corridor, then the next one after that, until finally…

To my astonishment, about twenty feet ahead of me lies a door. I feel this is it. I don't know why really. I have seen similar doors in this place before, only to be disappointed by what lies beyond. But this one feels different. I know it is. My heart is beating very fast. This is what will lead me back to my existence; to my life. This is my escape. And I have waited long enough for this moment. It's just ahead of me. I feel myself shaking with excitement. Please don't let me down. Please don't. I want this all to end. I race toward the door as fast as my legs will carry me. Another thought of my mother comes to me. This is a thought of what is to come. This time she is smiling and laughing. I can't wait to jump up out of bed and give you the biggest hug. I miss you, mommy. I'm coming back. Your baby boy is coming back to you, mommy.

Chapter 15

Interlude 3: Finality

The drive to the hospital is a familiar one for Sarah. The days and nights she has spent there are too numerous to count. The usual conversations she has on her drive are ones that only take place to herself in her head. Today is not usual, however. Jackie has agreed to drive her to the hospital, knowing full well the condition Sarah would be in after the day's events. Sarah considers Jackie to be a good friend, and she is glad that she will be there by her side when this all plays out.

The conversations this day are filled with stories of the past. They are stories Sarah holds dear to her heart; of better days when her beautiful baby boy was young and enthusiastic, and funny, and so full of life. She tells Jackie of the time when Daniel was four years old and he was so afraid to step on an anthill for fear he was killing off an entire kingdom of them. Or the time they went to the beach, and Daniel walked up to a very obese man sunbathing, pointed at him, and yelled back to her "Mom, is this a whale?" It was embarrassing at the time, but now she thinks back and smiles in contentment at his innocence. Her baby boy was such a joy. She feels her demeanor change to happiness whenever she gets the opportunity to open up to someone about these past remembrances. They are far and few between, but she takes these moments in stride and lets her heart feel an instance of bliss.

Similar stories unfold. Little tidbits of past joys are shared. Laughter is mingled in with stints of tears. And because of it, the drive to the hospital doesn't seem to take long enough for Sarah. She knows that the sooner they arrive, the sooner her world will be shattered and she will never be the same. But as inevitabilities happen, arrive they do, and Sarah can't help the overwhelming feeling of dread come upon her.

"Can we just sit here for a moment?" Sarah asks. "I just need a moment. I miss him so much; my dear sweet boy Daniel. What I wouldn't give to have him back with me; even for just five minutes. I want to tell him how much I love him. To hear him laugh again; cry, sing, scream; all of it. I just miss it so much. I miss *him*."

Jackie looks to Sarah, "Of course we can sit here," She replies. "Take what time you need. We'll wait until you are ready."

"Thank you, Jackie. I don't know what I would do if you weren't here with me. How does any parent let their child go like this?"

Jackie pauses for a moment, thinking of the right words to say. "This is a difficult situation, but one I think is necessary. You must be able to go forward and move on with your life. I think you know that too. Deep down, you need for this to happen to let Daniel go and be in peace. And you know in time, the healing will begin for you. He will always be here with you. You've shown me that in the stories you've told me. He will forever be in your heart, and he will be watching over you from afar. But it is time for that process to start. You will get through this. And today is the first step. It's a big first step. But you are so very brave for taking it."

With tears rolling down her cheek, Sarah reaches over and pulls Jackie into a big hug. She realizes she squeezes a bit tighter than usual this time, yet somehow she just can't relax her grip. She knows Jackie will understand. A minute passes before the women release from their embrace. Sarah's eyes, puffy and bloodshot, continue to expel liquid emotion while she attempts to compose herself. She wipes her eyes with her sleeves and brushes her hair back from her face with her palms, knowing full well that nobody would expect her to look her best this morning. She turns her attention once more toward the hospital, draws in a deep breath, and then states in a heavy, labored voice…

"I'm ready."

It is a lie really, for how could anybody be ready to let their child go like this. But she knows what Jackie told her about moving forward and healing is also very true. Daniel has been virtually lifeless for six years, lying in that bed unresponsive, and Sarah has been there night and day by his side. She has, for the most part, put her life on hold, always waiting for him to finally awaken. But now, these past few months, it has only been the machines hooked to his young body that have been truly keeping him alive. Her son will never again open his eyes. He will never look up at her and smile that beautiful smile of his. She will never get to hear his voice again. She won't get to hear him tell her that he loves her anymore. She knows this. The guilt she feels has practically consumed her. Not a day goes by that she doesn't punish herself with thoughts of "what ifs." What if she didn't get him a new bicycle? She never should have let him ride his bike alone. If she was out there with him, maybe none of this would have happened. It is all torture to her, and it will continue on long past today.

The condition he is in now; his current state; also weighs heavily on her conscience. She has played the conversations with the doctors and nurses over and over in her head. And she has blamed herself too many times for leaving him to go to Florida for work. She understands what happened was not her fault. Even if she had been present that day that her baby boy had sat up in his bed, things would have inevitably ended up the same way. There's nothing she could have done to change anything. She has come to grips with that reality now. It is time to finally let

Daniel go be in peace. And it is time for her to finally find her peace with it as well. Not that she ever will.

As she slowly walks through the hallways of the hospital, she feels the eyes of every person peering at her. Perhaps they are shaming her for her decision. Maybe they are offering up their heartfelt remorse. In reality, it doesn't matter. It is just the thoughts swirling around in her head that make her think this way. It is only her shameful guilt that plays with her emotions. She is the only one judging her actions today. It is all she can do to keep from becoming sick to her stomach, but still, she presses forward.

With Jackie by her side being a sturdy post for which to lean on, they make their way to the room that has been her son's prison for a great deal of his life. As they enter, Sarah is surprised to see a woman standing at Daniel's bedside, intently staring down at him. Having heard the two women enter, the woman by Daniel's side quickly turns her attention to Sarah. The streak of white in her hair immediately gives her identity away. It is Sheila, another nurse that works in this ward. Sarah didn't recognize her at first since she rarely ever sees her during the times she visits. She also finds it quite strange to see her here in Daniel's room today; dressed in plain clothes, rather than the usual scrubs she is accustomed to seeing.

"Sheila," Jackie blurts out. "What are you doing here today? I thought you had the day off."

With a startled look on her face, Sheila begins to make her way toward the exit.

"I'm sorry," she says, as she approaches Sarah.

Just as she is about to pass by the two women, Sheila grabs Sarah's hand and looks into her eyes. The look of trepidation on Sheila's face sends a cold chill straight through Sarah's being. She can't help but feel that Sheila wants to say something. Instead, the nurse glances over at Jackie, then back to Sarah, and releases her hand. She then hastily departs the room, leaving Sarah to ponder what that was all about. It was all very strange and somewhat ominous.

"What was Sheila doing here?" Sarah asks.

"I don't know," Jackie replies. "She was probably just here to check her schedule or something."

"You don't suppose she was looking for me, do you?" Sarah adds. "I mean, she was in this room. She probably knows I was coming here today. I should go and find her. It doesn't make sense. And the way she left…"

"If she wanted to speak to you, she would have said something before she left. I'm sure it's nothing. Daniel has been in her care for a long time too, she was probably just saying her goodbyes. She just didn't want to add any unnecessary guilt or doubt to your already heavily burdened mind."

"You're probably right," Sarah says. "But she looked so afraid. It was kind of eerie."

Sarah turns her attention to her son, his chest rising and lowering with the timing of the ventilator. It is so quiet in this room compared to the rest of the hustle and bustle outside the door, but Sarah picks up on every little noise around her. Her senses heightened at this moment, she hears each beep of the heart monitor explode in her ear. She feels the vibration of the ventilator as it forces air into Daniel's lungs, and then hears the hissing sound as it draws the same air out. Even the clock on the wall has found a way to make sure that each tick of its hands bangs into her skull like a jackhammer. She is a little on edge at this moment, but she is by Daniel's side, and he will help her get through this. She stands by his bed and reaches for his hand. She feels its warmth as she grasps it ever so gently. How can this have happened, she thinks? How did it come to this? Why must this be…?

Jackie interrupts Sarah's thoughts, "I'm going to go find the doctor. There will be some paperwork that you will need to fill out, but don't worry about any of that right now. You sit with Daniel. There is no rush. Take all the time you need. Doctor Stevens will be in shortly to discuss things further with you."

"Thank you," Sarah says somberly. "Thank you so much for everything."

Jackie leaves Sarah to her thoughts. She then sits by his side, this young boy who has over these past six years become a young man. Still holding his hand, Sarah begins talking to him as if he was sitting up pleasantly listening to her. Tears begin to pour from her swollen eyes. She leans forward and kisses the back of his hand, and then gently rests her head on it. She begins to explain to Daniel how much she loves him and that she is doing this so that he can finally rest, and he can finally go be with his father. She asks him to forgive her and hopes that he understands. She tells him that she will think of him every day and that he will always be her "bestest little man." There are also moments of silence where Sarah lets her mind reflect on better days when she and Daniel would have a movie night, and eat popcorn together. She thinks of the times they would play board games some nights before his bedtime. She thinks of the nights she would sit reading to him from his favorite book. And she thinks about the times he would ask about his father, and how sad she felt that he never had the opportunity to meet him.

These thoughts will surely keep coming to her in the days and months to come, she thinks to herself, but she knows they are what will keep him with her. She will never forget or let go of any of the memories. Daniel will live on through her.

At that moment, the door opens, and the doctor enters the room, followed closely by Jackie. Sarah sits up and hurriedly wipes the tears from her cheeks. She takes comfort that the doctor politely nods to her to indicate that it is quite alright. He pulls up a chair beside her and shows to her a sorrowful smile. After several seconds of silence, he begins to explain to Sarah the next steps, and what will happen after the deed has been done. He explains to her the preparations that have been made in which the hospital will handle the body on her behalf and the paperwork that needs to be filled out before her leaving today. In truth, she is only partially paying attention to what the doctor is saying, as her brain is in such turmoil that she can't fully gather her wits. She knows Jackie will be there to help her understand things she may have missed.

When the doctor is finished, he gets up from the chair and tells Sarah to once again take what time she needs to say goodbye and to have Jackie come and get him when she is ready. Jackie sits in the chair no longer occupied by the doctor and clasps Sarah's hand. They both sit quiet and motionless just staring forward at Daniel. No words need to be spoken at this time. Sarah has nothing left inside of her to let out. Her mind is spent; her body feels drained of all energy. She stands up from her chair, reaches forward with her arm to wrap around her son, and presses her forehead against his. After a minute, she softly kisses him on the forehead, then the cheek, and whispers a last "I love you."

She turns to Jackie and says, "It's time."

Jackie makes her way out of the room to retrieve the doctor once again.

On another plane of existence, Daniel finally reaches the door in which he feels will bring him back into the arms of his mother. He knows she has waited so long for him to return, and he can now grant her that wish. The doorknob within his hand, he glances back one final time to see where he has been and to appreciate the feeling he now has that he will be leaving it behind.

Back in the hospital room, Sarah, Jackie, and Doctor Stevens stand silently at the bedside of Daniel. Sarah finds herself clutching Jackie's hand as she watches the doctor reach for the machine that has been the apparatus of life to her baby boy for several months. And in an instant, it is done. The doctor flips the switch and turns the ventilator off. Sarah feels her heart tumble into her stomach. Unable to cry, she stares down at the floor. Her thoughts swirling, she promises to tell Daniel every day that she loves him. She begs for his forgiveness and hopes one day she will forgive herself. She then glances back up to Daniel in the bed. Sarah watches as a final collapse of her son's chest expels his last breath.

In that other place, without any further hesitation, Daniel turns the knob. Just as he opens the door, his body suddenly stiffens for the briefest of moments and then collapses lifelessly to the floor. Everything once again… goes dark.

Back in the hospital room, Doctor Stevens records the time of death at 12:17 pm.

Chapter 16

The Past Revisited

It's been two weeks since the funeral. I should think about getting myself back to work. Insurance only covers so much, and the bills that keep piling up aren't going to miraculously pay themselves. I do so appreciate how my work has allowed me the extra time off. I think they realized how much I needed it. But the time off just allows me to wallow in self-misery a little more each day. Work would be a good distraction for me. If nothing else, it would help keep me busy. I need to get back there if I am ever going to start healing. I'll never be able to move past this, but I need to learn to move forward.

I sip from my coffee, as the silence of the morning allows me to think about how each day seems to be a struggle lately. It's getting harder to get out of bed each morning. Getting dressed has become an annoying chore. I have to stop thinking this way. I have to start thinking of ways I can get myself motivated. I could do some cleaning. That's not motivation; more like torture. I could go for a hike, but I'm not *that* motivated yet. Then my thoughts begin to wander a bit. I wonder how the project in Florida has come along. I haven't heard about it from anyone at work, but they should be fully operational by now. Which reminds me, I should get around to unpacking the last of my stuff from that trip. I think I still have a small travel bag that has been sitting untouched in the closet. It's settled then, that's how this day will start.

I finish my coffee first and then head to the bedroom to set about the task I have assigned myself. This should keep my mind occupied for a bit. I pull out the bag from the closet and drag it to the bed, where I can at least sit while doing the unpacking. I pull out a few personal items and place them on the bed beside me. Next, I pull out a couple of pairs of shorts, a "Florida" t-shirt that I bought at a touristy gift shop, and my blue tank top that I've been looking all over for. When I reach in to grab my sandals that are at the bottom of the bag, my fingers grab hold of something the sandals are sitting on top of. It's a book. It's the book I would read to Daniel. It was his favorite. I thought I had lost it. I couldn't find it anywhere. It was in my bag the whole time. I feel a sudden rush of both sadness and joy come across me.

I rub my fingers across the textured cover and study the lines of the picture displayed. I think about how happy this book made Daniel feel as I would lie in bed with him reading it until he dozed off to sleep. It's only when I open it up to start flipping through the pages that I notice the stamp on the inside cover. It alerts me to the fact that this book is not my book at all. This book belongs to the library in Florida that the sweet old man at the book store went out of his way to retrieve for me. In my haste, I must have thrown it in my bag when I packed up everything. I wasn't thinking straight at all. My only thought was to get back here as quickly as possible.

That damn phone call. Why then? Why at all? I should have been by his side. What was I thinking about going to Florida? I could have turned it down. I *should* have turned it down. If I had been with Daniel, maybe he...

I stop myself there. I've done this too many times already and it's always the same. I'm just beating myself up for nothing. I know there's nothing I could have done. I still would have received a phone call. I just would have been closer. That's the only difference.

I take in a deep breath and gather my thoughts back to the here and now. I focus back on the book sitting on my lap. I feel horrible now. The shop owner must think I stole it. I've got to send this back to him. I guess I now know what my next chore will be after I put my things away. It is strange, though, why I can't find *my* copy of the book anywhere. I'm sure it will turn up.

After getting my clothes organized and my personals put away, I grab the book and make my way back out into the kitchen. I know I had that store's business card here somewhere. I ruffle through the clutter in my junk drawer until I happen upon it. I'm glad I didn't throw it out. Now that I have the address, I'm going to package the book up and get it into the mail today. I think that sweet man will be quite happy to get it back.

I decide it's time to jump in the shower. This is a good thing. I didn't even take a shower yesterday. I didn't do much at all. I must be a mess. I step into the bathroom and look in the mirror to confirm what I already surmised. I look so pale. My hair is sticking in all directions. My eyes look swollen from the tears that I continue to cry each night. My cheeks are droopy, and my lips are chapped. Oh yeah, I look really lovely. I'm not even sure a shower will fix this. But it's a start. I turn the shower on to let it warm up, then look back once again at myself in the mirror. My mind shifts to Daniel for a moment, and how awful he looked in those final moments before the doctor...

He too was so very pale. And his body was so thin and frail-looking. It's not how I would like to remember him.

My thoughts snap back to me in the present, the visible steam indicating that the shower is ready for me. I disrobe and step into the water with the hope that it will wash all my troubles away. It won't, I know, but at the very least I'll feel a little cleaner than I have in the last couple of days.

After the shower, I quickly throw on some clothes and work my hair into something manageable. It's not the best look, but it'll do. I head back out into the kitchen where I left the book, and a thought jumps into my head. Today is Thursday. Jackie doesn't work on Thursdays. I should call her and see if she would like to meet me for an early lunch. I haven't heard from her since the funeral. It would be nice to sit and chat with her. I need someone other than myself to keep me company. I'm not sure I'm ready for anyone else just yet, but Jackie is different. She's been with me through most of this. She feels like my only family now.

I call her cell phone, but it goes directly to voice mail. I'll just leave her a message.

"Hi Jackie, it's Sarah. I haven't spoken with you in a while, and I was hoping maybe we could get together for lunch today. It would be great to see you. Call me back."

I hope she can. I miss our conversations, and I think it would be helpful for me. Honestly, I thought I would have heard from her before today. The hospital must be keeping her quite busy. No matter. I'll head out to the Post Office, and she'll get back to me when she can. It will be great to hear from her and what's going on in her world at the hospital though. I know it's strange, but I think in a way I miss the hospital. For six years it was kind of my second home. But at the same time…

I grab my jacket, the book, and my keys, and I step out to begin my short little jaunt. For the first time in a couple of weeks, I feel myself smile as I think about how returning this book will probably surprise the bookstore owner. It feels so good to smile.

The drive to the Post Office is surprisingly uneventful. There isn't as much traffic as I expected, and everything seems so calm and peaceful. I get to my destination in very little time. Unfortunately, the ease of this trip is about to end as I notice the line that has formed inside. I think I found out where everybody is. But since I don't have anything else to do, or anywhere else to go at the moment, it doesn't seem to bother me at all.

I grab a box suitable to package the book in, and I take my place at the back of the line. As I stand here, slowly inching forward with each person's dismissal from the counter, I feel everyone's eyes burning holes in me as they pass by. They all know, don't they? They are shaming me; judging me. But they aren't. Not really. I'm just feeling anxious about being around people. It's all in my mind. I just need to relax my thoughts.

I think once again back to Jackie. I hope she can meet me today. If not this early, then perhaps later this afternoon will work. It would be a nice welcome to the day.

The line steadily creeps forward until I finally find myself at the counter. The kindly postal employee helps me package the book and gets it all set to be shipped out. I feel a little relieved now knowing that soon it will be on its way back to its rightful place in the library from which it came.

Still not having heard from Jackie, I guess I will just return home until I can figure out what else I feel up to for today. Getting outside like this was a nice distraction. Maybe I'll think of something else to do out and about this afternoon if I don't get that call.

The trip back home is equally as quick and pain-less. As I approach my house, I notice a vehicle parked in my driveway, and a woman standing by my front door. I recognize her easily enough. It is Sheila, the nurse from the hospital. A lump in my throat im-mediately forms as I instinctively think the worst. What is she doing here? Has something happened to Jackie? I work to try to calm my mind and think in-stead that perhaps I may have just forgotten some-thing at the hospital that is being returned to me.

After parking, I step out to greet Sheila, and to ascertain her reason for being here. Her demeanor appears very rigid, and she has a very stoic look at the moment that doesn't seem to change as I make my way over to her.

"Hello, Sheila. Is there something I can help you with?"

She hesitates for a moment and then speaks.

"I need to talk to you about something, Sarah. It's important. Can we go inside and sit for a bit?"

Feeling somewhat confused, but also a little curious, I agree to welcome her inside to discuss what it is that is so important. I hope Jackie is ok. I start to feel a nervous sensation come upon me. My hands begin to tremble a little bit. I try my best to not let Sheila notice.

Once inside, I offer her a drink, which she refuses. It's for the best, as I probably would have spilled it with my hands shaking so much. I watch as Sheila oddly glances around the room as if looking for an appropriate place to sit. I can tell she seems a bit nervous being here, and I try to reassure her that she can relax.

"It's ok, sit wherever you'd like," I try to say calmly, but I'm sure my nerves show through.

"Thank you," she responds reservedly.

I decide to start the conversation to alleviate the tension surrounding this moment.

"So, Sheila, what brings you here? What's so important?"

No sooner do the words leave my lips than my guest blurts out her words without any further hesitation.

"Have you talked to Jackie? Have you seen her? I doubt you have. And I'm guessing you won't either."

I'm taken aback by this sudden barrage. Have my worries about Jackie's well-being been realized? I feel the urge to interrupt.

"Whoa! Slow down there? What's going on? Has something happened to Jackie?" I realize my voice has become elevated.

"I don't know," Sheila responds. "I don't know if anything has happened to her. I just know that she's gone."

"What… what do you mean 'she's gone?'" I interject.

"I mean she hasn't been back to work since your son's funeral. Nobody has heard from her at all. I tried calling her several times, but all I'd gotten was her voicemail. After a few days, I went to check on her to see if she was all right, and she wasn't home. Her car was there, but she didn't answer the door. I went a few more times after that, and each time, it was the same thing. Her neighbor was outside the last time I went to her place and he told me that she hasn't been around at all."

"I've tried to call her too," I let Sheila know. "Could she have maybe gone on vacation or something? Maybe she's with family?" I say these things, but in my head, I am so confused. Selfishly, I think why would Jackie just leave me?

Sheila continues, "I checked with the hospital, and she didn't have any vacation time planned on the calendar. I got a little worried, so I called the police to explain the situation. They couldn't do anything since she is an adult, and nobody has filed a formal missing person's report. They suggested I check with the other local hospitals, which I did, and still had no luck. So yesterday, I decided to go back to her house again to check on her. I was determined to find out what was going on. I knocked on her door, and as with every other time, she didn't answer. I called her phone again just in case, and again it sent me right to voicemail. I couldn't see into any of her windows, as they all seemed to have blinds on them that were closed.

"I went over to her neighbor's house and explained what was going on and how I was worried about her. I asked if he wouldn't mind accompanying me as a witness while I tried some of her windows to see if any were unlocked. I also expressed to him that I may have to break a window to get in if none were. He was a bit hesitant, but he agreed. As luck would have it, one of her rear windows was unlocked, and as soon as we opened it, we could smell a pungent odor. Working in a hospital, you get used to the smell of certain things; death and decay; disease and rotting flesh; after a while, your senses become numb to it. But this was something different; something more.

"Even more concerned now, her neighbor helped me up to get inside. I told him to go back around to the front and I would unlock the door. He told me he didn't feel comfortable going inside, but that he would stay out in front and wait for me.

"Have you ever been to Jackie's house, Sarah?"

"No, I haven't. We mostly only spent time with each other at the hospital. Although, shortly before Daniel... well... near the end, she had visited me a few times here. Why?"

"When I got into her house, I was standing in the kitchen. Besides the god-awful stench, there was a coldness in the air that chilled me to the bone. I could see my breath when exhaling. Also, everything was just black. And I don't mean because the lights were off. I had turned them on to see. I mean *everything* was black. The walls; the floor; the ceiling; everything was covered in some type of black paint or something. As I made my way into the next room, I could see that there was no furniture anywhere. I called out Jackie's name, but I got no response. Then as I slowly walked down her hallway toward another room, I could see something painted in white on the door ahead of me. There were some sort of symbols, or pictures, or something. I can't even explain it. I could feel my breathing becoming shallower, and my heart was pounding as I reached for the doorknob. I was imagining the worst beyond the door, expecting Jackie to be lying dead on the floor in some kind of awful condition. I almost couldn't bring myself to do it, but felt I had to find out for sure. So I collected myself and I opened the door.

"Jackie was not there. But Sarah..., what I saw in that room; on the walls; is the reason why I am here today. Every inch of the walls had your son's name carved into them. 'Daniel' was everywhere. It gave me a feeling of such overwhelming dread. I couldn't stay inside there any longer, and I ran for the front door. The neighbor was still outside as he said he would be, but I couldn't even stop to say anything to him. I just had to get out of there as fast as I could. I just got into my car and drove off."

At this point, I am utterly shocked at what Sheila has told me, and I can see by her trembling hands that she is shaken up as well. None of this makes any sense to me. I feel like I am going to throw up. I keep swallowing hard as my mouth fills with saliva. Still, I have to ask.

"What was Daniel's name doing on the walls? I mean, why would anybody carve someone's name into their walls? What the hell is going on? I'm calling Jackie right now." My demeanor is starting to show the anger building inside of me.

"You won't get her," I hear Sheila say as I dial the number. "She's not here anymore."

Once again the call goes directly to voicemail. I leave another message. This one is a little more pointed.

"Jackie, what the hell is going on? Are you ok? Do you have my son's name on your walls? Why? I need to know what is going on! What is happening? You need to call me back!"

I hang up the phone and look back toward Sheila, who in turn, is just staring at me with frightened eyes.

"Why do you keep saying I won't reach her, and that she's not here? Do you know anything else? Tell me, damn it!" I now realize I am yelling.

Sheila begins again. "I drove off from her house terrified. I never felt that way in my life. Something evil was in that house, and now that I was away from it, my thoughts began to clear a little. I suddenly was filled with thoughts from a few months back, at the hospital. I was there, you know. That night your son awoke."

"I know you were," I replied. "Jackie told me. But you had left before that happened."

"No, I was the nurse on duty that night. I was taking care of Daniel when Jackie came in to tell me that I was needed in another room. She told me she would continue rubbing Daniel's muscles while I was away. I thought it was a bit strange, to be taken out of his care at this time, but I did as she asked.

"As I headed down the hall, a couple of security officers ran past me toward a commotion that was taking place a few rooms ahead of me. Another security officer stopped me from continuing forward and turned me away. He said that for my safety I shouldn't come any closer. As it turns out, that was the room Jackie had stated I was needed in. It looked like security had things under control. Once things appeared to calm down, I made my way back to Daniel's room.

"When I got there I stopped in the doorway shocked at what I was witnessing. Jackie and Doctor Stevens were both in the room, and your son was sitting up in bed shouting out some words I didn't understand. Then he stopped, and I swear he turned his head to look right at me. He then started yelling toward me, 'I am here. Save me. Help! I am here.' Then he turned even further to look at Jackie, and he raised his arm and pointed right at her, before continuing to yell some more words that I didn't understand. He began shaking and convulsing violently. Jackie noticed me standing in the doorway and yelled to me to go and get an orderly. I did as she asked, but by the time we had returned to the room, Daniel was lying motionless again and the doctor was checking his vitals.

"Jackie pulled me out into the hall and asked me how much I had seen. I told her I saw the whole incident. It was frightening. She told me not to say anything to you about this and that she would explain what had happened. But now, after having been in Jackie's house and seeing that room, I think your son was truly asking for my help that night."

"For your help?" I notice my voice has risen a bit. "Help for what? What are you telling me?"

"What I am telling you, Sarah, is that I think your son was asking for my help from her; from Jackie. He looked right at me, clear as day, and he asked for my help. Then he looked at her, and he pointed right at her as if to tell me that he needed saving from her. I know it sounds crazy, but her house had a stench worse than death inside. And everything was covered in black. And there were those strange symbols painted on her door. And after the feeling I had when

I saw those walls; and Daniel's name carved all over them; it brought me right back to that night. I know I'm right. And the fact that she has been missing since your son's funeral... she's gone. And I think she has taken your son from you."

At that moment, a realization pierces through me. Jackie was the one who first suggested I let Daniel go be in peace. I begin shaking, and tears begin to roll down my cheeks.

"Why would she do this?" I ask. "What kind of person would do this?"

"I've been thinking this through all night, Sarah. I don't think Jackie was the person we all thought she was. I can't help but feel... maybe she wasn't what any of us could have thought she was"

I try to come up with words between the sobbing.

"What are you talking about, Sheila? What are you saying? Who the hell was she then?"

Chapter 17

Darkness Prevails

She is pleased with her work. She knows that she has once again managed to diminish the hopes of these people a little further. Each light extinguished only helps weaken the barrier she so fervently wants to break asunder. She relishes in the knowledge that her kind's darkness strengthens with each failed attempt by those wretched angels to restore light and order. Her ilk is not about maintaining order. They perpetuate chaos and ruin. They feed on fear and hopelessness and destruction and the heartache of those tortured souls left behind to feel the effects of

241

the devastation they have wrought. She is a Dark Queen; a demon of the highest order. She will stop at nothing to ensure darkness prevails. She knows this latest victory; one that has taken many years to accomplish; will leave lingering effects on those closest to the life she was finally able to quench. There is now a seed of darkness planted within the living that will continue to fester and grow until it consumes the very essence of its host. This has ever been her plan. She understands complete domination takes time.

Though this Dark Queen is more powerful than the lesser demon lackeys under her command, even she does not have the power to take a mortal life. Just as her angel counterparts do not have the power to resurrect a life. Both warring factions of good and evil can merely 'push' people in a direction. They can only manipulate a person's actions by preying on the individual's doubts and weaknesses. The disgusting humans were granted free will oh so long ago, to decide their miserable fates. This is a misfortune that cannot be overcome. Only *they* can make the final decisions that will impact their meager existence. But with all things, there are ways around certain complications. And both the forces of light and dark do what they can to sway the very souls they oversee to help tip the scales in their favor.

The angels have always held the upper hand. In sheer numbers alone, they are at a great advantage. Their sphere of influence is powerful, and the ease in which they have been able to persuade the humans into doing what's right has been impressive. But over time, they have gotten too relaxed; too confident in their abilities. Perhaps they have given the weak species they protect too much credit. Nevertheless, the demons, in their ever-increasing lust for control and ascendancy, have discovered the means to change all that. They have become a more formidable force than the angels have given them credit for. Directed by the order of Dark Queens, the demon hordes seek out not only the individuals they plan to destroy from within, but also those around them to enlist in their efforts.

It isn't enough to take advantage of a single being's inner turmoil. The presence of darkness can grow deeper and spread like a disease when many others are infected with the same fears and insecurities. The demons also know that there is much more damage inflicted when toying with each victim's emotions; giving them hope; only to tear them down until there is nothing left but misery and shame. This helps feed into the satisfaction the demons get when tormenting the unsuspecting souls they lay claim to. Such was the case in this latest successful mission.

Undoubtedly, she will take all the credit for this triumph, but in truth, she had underlings helping to do her bidding. Like the angels, who are sent out in pairs as pawns for righteousness, she too has her obedient pets to deploy on behalf of her sinister assignment. They have been most useful to her on countless occasions. She delights in the thought of how cunning and devious they are. She calls upon them now so that they may reunite and revel in this most wicked of achievements. When the Dark Queen summons them, there is no hesitation in response, for fear of utter annihilation. In an instant, they are by her side; these two lowly demons; Ygdarmisalenth and the one called Mr. Greeg.

"You summoned us, my queen?" Ygdarmisalenth inquires. "You are satisfied with our work, are you not?"

This Dark Queen looks at her two recruits, who upon their arrival immediately dropped to their knees in obedience, and snarls at them in gratitude. With her black, forked tongue, she licks away a stream of slaver that begins dripping from her lips.

"You have done well my children. I am pleased with your efforts. Another soul is lost to the dark. Share with me the details of how it is you made your unsuspecting victim suffer to his very core."

Mr. Greeg anxiously chimes in. "It worked like a charm. We had this kid believing we were our hated enemies. It was fun playing with his tender emotions. The more innocent they are, the more satisfied I feel."

"What Mr. Greeg is trying to say," Ygdarmisalenth adds, "is that it is quite a delicious treat feeding off of these creatures' ignorance. They don't even have the wherewithal to understand that the confusion they feel is a direct result of our inter-action with them. They are but insects to be toyed with and tortured until their inevitable end. And this boy; this Daniel; was no exception. Although I must say, he was quite a little fighter, that one. We took great pleasure in breaking him down."

"Yes, we did." Mr. Greeg continues. "I even got to put a lashing on the boy so he could feel some real pain. I beat him and whipped him bloody. And then when he would heal, I would do it all over again. It was a delight to watch as the metal barbs of my whip would cut into the child's flesh. The blood would trickle down from the gaping wounds making my mouth water. I could taste that red liquid in the air. I could taste his anguish. I could taste his fear. In that place in his mind, that dark place he retreated to, he never remembered the torture as much as I would have liked. But it wasn't the physical pain I was interested in anyway. It was the emotional scars left behind that never quite heal. And when the physical abuse stopped, that's when the real enjoyment started."

Ygdarmisalenth jumps in, "Humans have such fragile psyches. It's not difficult to twist their thoughts and manipulate them in all kinds of deceitful ways. This pitiful Daniel had so many jumbled thoughts in his head. The Edward persona he took on for instance; that was unexpected. Perhaps it was a defense mechanism? No matter. It was easy to make him see whatever it was we wanted him to see. Making him believe, however, was a different matter entirely. He struggled to make sense of what we were showing and telling him, fighting us every step of the way. I must say, although he was more of a challenge than most we have encountered, it made it that much more rewarding in the end. Still, it did take quite a bit of time. Maybe it was a bit too much. After all, Mr. Greeg here was starting to burn through his host body. If that had happened, and his true appearance had been revealed, we may have lost Daniel right then and there."

Mr. Greeg excitedly interrupts. "Oh, that's when you whispered to me. That was very clever of you to play with Daniel's head that way. The way you tapped into his thoughts and made him think your hand was glowing like you were one of those disgusting angels hit it home for him I think. He was so gullible. You should have seen his face."

"Yes well, anyway," Ygdarmisalenth continues, "it played out perfectly. And so did your plan, my queen. Your timing was impeccable, as always. How you convinced this child's mother to give up on her only son, and ultimately send him to his bitter end, was something only one such as yourself could have pulled off."

The Queen sneers at Ygdarmisalenth's comment, and her eyes narrow, as a look of repugnance comes across her face.

"You had better restrain your condescending words, lackey. My 'timing' as you put it, was calculated. Mr. Greeg's weakness is on him. And although I do enjoy hearing about the physical torture Daniel was subjected to, that could have ruined everything. Had the boy died before his wretched mother could kill him, then Mr. Greeg would have learned firsthand what real torture felt like for all eternity. My agenda was carefully and deliberately planned to its fruition. Sarah had to be torn apart from the inside so that she could fully carry the guilt that now resides within her. She will start to negatively impact all those she is connected to, as she slowly begins to wither away. Darkness spreads, and eventually, it overcomes and consumes."

The two lesser demons grin at their master's words. Mr. Greeg, still excited about their accomplishment, can't contain himself from speaking further.

"My favorite part was when Ygdarmisalenth had the boy believing he was going to make it out of that forsaken place he was in. He practically showed Daniel the way and everything. Daniel had such high hopes of making it back to his mother; we could smell it emanating from his pores. And then, when the opening was right there in front of him, and all he had to do was step through it, all hope was immediately shattered. It was truly wicked."

"Yes, that is true, Mr. Greeg," Ygdarmisalenth states. "It was exhilarating to watch the boy's lifeless body limply collapse to the ground just as he was about to be free from his subconscious prison. But I am curious about something, my queen. What about the book you confiscated from the boy's room. Whatever was that for, and what became of it?"

The Demon Queen glares at her two underlings with disdain before deciding to answer Ygdarmisalenth's inquiry.

"The book you speak of contained things that gave the boy hope. And with hope, there is a glimmer of light. I could not allow Sarah to read from it any longer. Had she continued to read it to Daniel, he may have garnered enough strength to find his way back sooner than anticipated. I would not let that happen. So I took it from her possession and I destroyed it, so that no others may read from it and begin to build hope from the story contained within its pages."

Once the three harbingers of darkness have finished with the exchange of their malevolent chronicles, the Dark Queen signals for her two evil minions to fall in line and follow along behind her. The day is young, and there is still much to do. She has already broken through to the disgusting realm that is Elsewhere. If she is to be the first demon to break through to the great kingdom beyond, she knows the darkness must grow ever darker. She knows, in time, it will cast its shroud over all of humanity. But for now, there are other souls out there needing to be snatched away from the grasp of the hated angels and their penchant for good and light. The demons are getting stronger. With each rotting human soul taken by her kind, the angels weaken and will soon bow down to her and her evil brethren. With that knowledge burned deep into her thoughts, the three demons depart; off to claim their next tormented soul.

Chapter 18

Glimmer

Today is no different than any other average morning. For much of the past thirty-four years, the routine has been the same. Start the day with a nice light breakfast, take in the morning's fresh air, and then stroll the two blocks to the place where he finds comfort and solace. After the brief jaunt, taking great care to stop at the produce stand along the way to grab an orange, which has become a favorite practice of his, the old man arrives at his destination.

Yes, today is no different than any other average morning, except that this morning, as he opens the front door to the place that has become like a second home to him, it does not just swing open revealing the morning's mail as it travels easily over the envelopes dropped in from the mail slot above. Instead, he feels the door hit an obstacle as it pushes open. His immediate thought is that he must have dropped something inside the night before as he made his way out and locked up for the night.

The kindly, old man enters through the door to find a small package that has been delivered along with the mail. By its size, it is easy for the man to determine the package's contents without having to open it. Still, he picks up the box and the remaining pieces of mail at his feet and then closes the door behind him. He turns the sign hanging in the window over from "Closed" to "Open," and then makes his way over to the counter, where he can get a peek at this surprising package delivered to him. It's not that he isn't accustomed to packages being delivered to him. It's rather a regular occurrence for his business. He receives shipments every couple of weeks; sometimes even twice in one week. But those are much larger boxes and also expected since he places the orders for those specific items. But he has placed no orders this week, so this particular package is an unusual surprise to him.

Even at his advanced age, he still gets a feeling of excitement as he opens each shipment that arrives for him. The joy he feels as he opens each box to reveal the wondrous contents within. The smell of the freshly printed volumes of the latest bestsellers never disappoints his senses. He delights in unpacking each tome as he studies their beautifully crafted covers, imagining the fantastical stories waiting within for all who wish to release its magnificent mysteries. And although he knows this package that lies in front of him contains but a single book, he can't help but feel just a bit more excited than usual.

He tears open the flap of the postal carton and slides out the package from within. It is a book, just as he had suspected. Accompanying the book is a handwritten note that reads:

"Thank you very much for your efforts in securing this book for me. I'm very sorry that it took so long to get this back to you. It has meant a great deal to me and has helped me immensely through a difficult time. It was much appreciated. All the best."

He turns the book over to reveal its cover and is at once taken back to many months earlier when a young woman came into his store asking for this book. After all this time, he had forgotten about it.

But now seeing it once again, he recalls the memory as if it had just happened the day before.

He remembers the young woman being anxious and a bit distraught. He recollects the story she told him about her son and the appalling tragedy that had befallen him. He thinks about how this book was the child's favorite book because it reminded him of his father; a father he had never met. The woman explained to him about how the boy's father had died in the war efforts shortly before their son was born, but that she would tell her son all about his father and how strong and brave he was.

He was truly a kind-hearted man who put all others above himself, which is why he had decided to join the military. It was because of his strong sense of devotion to his country, and the willingness to want to help protect his fellow man. Soon after, she learned she was pregnant. She knew how overjoyed her husband was to hear the news, and he couldn't wait to get back to her to bring their child into the world together. It was during her pregnancy that the government had begun to deploy the armed forces overseas. Her husband's unit was no exception, and he soon found himself in a far-off land embroiled in a foreign war. It would be several months later that she would learn of the unfortunate death of her husband,

and suddenly hit with the realization that she would have to raise their child on her own. She felt greatly saddened that her son would have to grow up without his father, and never knowing what a wonderful man he was, but she was determined to let him know every chance she could. She wanted her little boy to be proud of his dad, and to know that even though he never had the opportunity to meet him, that he would have been loved more than anything else in the world.

One day, when her son was just five years old, they were in a book store much like this one, when the boy happened upon a book that caught his attention. His eyes were immediately drawn to it because he noticed the title of the book had his father's name printed on it. He begged his mother to buy it for him, which of course she did. She realized the significance of the title and what it meant to the boy. She told the old man how she would read the book to her son each night, and how he would react to the story of the characters inside. The young boy would imagine the main character in the story was his father. They had the same name after all; the titular character and his dad; so it wasn't difficult to do. It was a marvelous story that played out magnificently on the pages. The brightly colored pictures within helped tell the tale of the many adventures the hero of the story would be involved in. Aided by his trusty companions, the titular character would help save the weak and less fortunate from the dastardly villains lurking about. The story would unfold magically before his young eyes. His mother would read from the book in a fashion that would brilliantly capture not only the splendid characterization but also the boy's inspired imagination. Through the story in this children's book, her son felt like he had a connection to his father, and therefore it meant everything to him. Even as the boy got a little older, the book remained his favorite. He still enjoyed the times his mother would read it to him, after which, she would tell him stories of his father, and how he was such a good man.

This emotional tale, told to him by the young mother, pulled at the shop keeper's heart-strings so deeply that he felt compelled to do all that he could to get a copy of this book for her. It is the very reason why he contacted other establishments and went out of his way to retrieve this children's book from a library a couple of towns over.

Sitting behind the counter, the book splayed in front of him, he studies the cover intently. His curiosity piqued, he begins perusing through the book, skimming through the artfully crafted story, and taking in the beautiful illustrations displayed on many of the pages. He can understand why the young boy appreciated this book as much as he did; if not just for the title. It is a fine piece of literary work.

He knows this is the library's copy, which he will make arrangements to return tonight after work, but he can't help think that this book would be a wonderful addition to his growing collection. It will be difficult since it is out of print, but he will investigate the possibility of getting some copies for his store's shelves. It is this type of story that sparks the imagination and instills hope and faith and courage into young children. The world is a dark enough place to grow up in, so having such an incredible book to bring a glimmer of light to a child in this ever-darkening world is something akin to a miracle.

He stares once again at the cover and traces his finger across the embossed lettering at the top. How proud the woman's son must have been to read his father's name exhibited in such bold letters atop this book. He can just imagine the boy's adoration to think that maybe, just maybe, his father was indeed the hero of the story. It is a testament of the love shared between a young boy and his father; even one he had never met.

A heartfelt smile splashes across this tender old man's face. He places the book down behind the counter and goes over to a nearby shelf to organize a little. He continues to think about the young mother, her son, and the unfortunate circumstances that led to him coming in contact with that book. And what an amazing little children's book it is;

"Edward and the Angels."

Epilogue

The More Things Change…

Sarah breathes in the salty air from the gentle breeze flowing off the morning ocean tide, as the waves rush in to meet the shoreline. She is relaxed. Her eyes closed, she feels the wind take hold of her hair and brush it across her shoulders. The sound of the waves rolling over each other gives her a calming sensation. The feel of the sand beneath her feet as she lets her toes mingle and play with the granules is soothing to her. Never could she have believed this would be her life. This is her new routine; her new "normal."

The early mornings are her favorite time of the day. They allow her to reflect upon the changes she has had to make in her life; the changes that were necessary for her to move on from her tragic past. These moments on the beach help calm her emotions and start her day on a positive note. No longer does she harbor the negativity inside that she felt for so long. She couldn't let those feelings devastate her any longer. They were eating her up from the inside and she was losing control of her life. She couldn't let that happen.

For the first year after she was manipulated into killing her son, Sarah was obsessed with finding out where Jackie was; *who* Jackie was. The startling news from Sheila just about broke her. The woman Sarah believed to be her friend was instead something much worse. Who she was; what she was; is still not clear to her, but Jackie was no doubt evil incarnate.

The obsession started as repeated phone calls to Jackie's cell phone. Soon the number was no longer in service. Then there were the trips to the hospital to question other staff members. In truth, "Question" is too innocent a word. She would chastise the employees quite regularly for having had any association with that awful woman. She knew they weren't to blame, but she couldn't help herself. Many times she would find herself forcibly removed by security. It was getting a little out of hand. And it didn't stop there either.

Her mind was constantly distracted by what had happened. She was riddled with guilt. She needed answers, and she knew the only person who could give them to her was the person she could no longer find. Her incessant behavior spilled into her professional life. She was constantly on the internet at work, searching for clues about who that dreadful woman was that stood by her side all those years. That terrible woman was in charge of her son's care. As difficult as Sarah was on those around her, she was always hardest on herself. How could she have been so foolish? How could she have let Jackie convince her to give up on her beautiful baby boy? Eventually, her work lapsed too much and mistakes were too frequent that her company was forced to let her go.

The worst thing she did, which sent her over the edge, was to visit that house; Jackie's house. After several inquiries and complaints to the police, they finally opened a missing person's case and investigated. They entered the home and found what Sheila had described, and then they immediately cordoned off the premises. Nobody was allowed access except for the police and forensics. But that wasn't going to stop Sarah. She needed to see for herself. She thought maybe there might be some clues inside that would lead to Jackie's whereabouts. She was desperate, distraught, and becoming mildly unhinged. The yellow "Do Not Cross" police tape wasn't going to prevent her from finding out the truth. She broke in one night, and it almost cost her everything.

She stood in the doorway at the end of the hall cringing at the sight of her son's name scratched into the walls. Emotions overtook her at that moment and she dropped to her knees sobbing uncontrollably. Staring at the walls in sheer terror, "Daniel" was carved into them everywhere you could see. The entire room was blanketed with his name. It was just like Sheila had described to her, only much worse now that she could see it for herself. Sarah somehow managed to get to her feet, and then stumbled her way back out of the house, never to return.

After that, Sarah's life began to spiral downward even more. She felt she had lost everything. First, she had lost her husband Edward to a war overseas. Then she had lost her son Daniel at her own hands. Her job was gone. The few friends she had left soon abandoned her due to her neurotic behavior. She lacked the motivation to do anything. After a while, she couldn't pay her bills. Any amount of savings she once had, had quickly diminished. It was only a matter of time until she lost her home too.

Then one night in a dream; or perhaps it was a vision; Daniel spoke to her. They were simple words.

"Mommy, I miss you. I need you to come back."

But they were enough. It was the sound of salvation from the lips of her sweet little boy.

If not for that one incredible moment, Sarah may not have come back from her inner turmoil. She wouldn't have decided right then and there that she needed to change her life. It was no longer only about herself, but the memory of her beautiful Daniel. His death was no longer going to be in vain. He wouldn't want her to go on destroying herself, so she was no longer going to let it.

There was nothing left for her in her old world, so she decided to leave it behind. She sold her house and moved down to Florida where she felt she needed to go to put closure on her negative feelings. It was here where she once was when she left her son for a short while. And it was here where she had received the horrible news about her son's condition. She knew it would be here where she would learn to heal.

Now she finds herself in a much better place. It has been six years since Daniel was laid to rest. He saved her. She knows that. She will never forget him. And more importantly, she has forgiven herself. It took some time, but she had help.

As she stands at the foot of the beach letting the water flood onto her feet, she places her hand on her belly to remind her of all she has to live for. This tender child growing inside her; this little girl; will be loved more than anything else.

"I won't let you down," Sarah whispers to herself as she shuffles her palm from side to side.

She is slightly distracted and doesn't hear the approaching footsteps from behind.

"Good morning, dear," the voice from behind her rings out. In her previous life, she may have been startled by such a disruption to her quiet concentration. These days, however, she is at peace with herself, and the words only comfort her.

"Good morning, my wonderful husband," Sarah responds.

"Well, to what do I owe that charming response?" her husband questions.

"I've just been thinking. I couldn't be happier than I am right now. You've been so supportive and wonderful. You've helped me so much. I love you, Michael. That's all."

"Wow. This pregnancy must be agreeing with you. You're beautiful, you know. And I love you too."

"Oh," Sarah jumps in, "while I've been enjoying the morning, I've also decided on a name for our little girl. Tell me what you think. Corinne."

"Hmm… Corinne. I think it's great. How about a middle name?"

"Well, I was thinking…," Sarah adds, "what about Danielle?"

Michael repeats the name a couple of times. "Corinne Danielle. Corinne Danielle. I think we can make it work."

"I'm glad you are ok with it," Sarah says. "How did I get so lucky to meet you? You truly are heaven-sent, Mr. Michael Greeg."

"Oh, come on now," Michael replies. "I'm most assuredly not heaven-sent. And there's no need to be so formal with me. You can simply call me 'Mr. Greeg.'"

And the two have a little laugh as they peer off into the ocean together.

Keep an eye out for more of The DARK Series.

The second novel is coming.

Read on for the first chapter of…

DARK LANE

Chapter 1

The Millers

"It's this Goddamn place." he used to say. "There's something wrong here." Bud Miller, a simple man who, after retiring, only wanted to take life each day as it came. He and his wife Martha owned a nice piece of property at the end of Helms Lane; a quiet little cul-de-sac. Their land stretched just about three acres, and Bud finally had the opportunity to concentrate on what he always dreamed of doing. He wanted to create a large garden with vegetable crops that would fully sustain their dietary needs. It would encompass the majority of their full acreage and would allow them to reap the complement of rewards during harvesting. This was some-

1

thing he always dreamed of doing since he was much younger.

Bud's father was a farmer in Indiana, and it was very important to him to pass this on to his son (the necessary skills for working the land so that one day he could take over the family business). Farming is not an easy job, but Bud was up for the challenge.

He was twelve years old when he was first allowed to drive the tractor all by himself. Even at a young age, it was a liberating feeling. He fell in love with it, and he fell in love with farming. For five years father and son worked the farm together. Bud felt content. This was everything he dreamed of doing and planned to continue after he got out of college. But sometimes dreams have to be put on a shelf for a while.

Bud was supposed to carry on the family tradition, but when he went off to college he met a young lady that he instantly fell in love with. Suddenly, farming didn't seem to matter as much anymore. This beautiful girl, Martha, was all he could think of and he knew he wanted to spend every waking moment with her.

Martha was from a well-to-do family in Washington, D.C. She was strong-willed and very independent, which often caused her to clash with her parent's ideas of what they wanted for her. Her parents wanted her to attend Georgetown University to focus on Political Science and Government. She had other plans. Out of spite more than anything else, or perhaps just plain rebellion, she went in another direction. Martha *did* attend Georgetown. Only, it was Georgetown College in Kentucky rather than Georgetown University in Washington. She decided to focus on Psychology and Women's Studies. It was while at Georgetown College that she met Bud Miller.

The two fell in love, and after graduating from college, were soon married. Martha wanted to move back to Washington where, despite her differences with her parents, she could be closer to family. Bud was agreeable to this and decided to forsake his dream of being a farmer like his father was before. It helped that, as a wedding gift, Martha's parents had planned to buy the newlyweds a house on the outskirts of the city. And so, to Washington, they went; and they settled nicely into their new residence at 44 Helms Lane.

It lay vacant for a time; this "cursed" property as Bud always called it. And with good reason too. Strange things seemed to start happening there shortly after he retired. They started as small things. Every once in a while there would be a light that would turn on by itself. At first, both Bud and Martha found it amusing. But after weeks of this happening at random times, they called in an electrician to look at the wiring. Unfortunately, the electrician couldn't find anything wrong. Everything seemed to be in order. So they were forced to live with the annoyance of the lights playing tricks. A short time later, and with no additional effort put forth by the married couple to correct it, the light situation seemed to fix itself, so it was no longer a concern. But then doors started opening and closing by themselves. The bedroom door would be open one moment then slam shut the next. The front door would be closed then suddenly burst open. The couple would attribute it to a cross-breeze that must have blown in from the windows that they would often have open. When the animated doors continued into the winter months when all the windows were closed, however, it became clear that something was very odd. Other unexplainable things too, began happening. A blender would turn on in the middle of the night startling the sleeping couple. The shower would turn on for no reason, and then just as quickly turn off. Something would fall off a shelf when no one was near it. The temperature in their home would suddenly drop to freezing for hours at a time. These sorts of things continued for almost two years. It was something like you would expect to see in a movie about a haunted house, only it wasn't a movie, and it was becoming very frightening. Many nights were spent roaming about the house checking out where the strange noises were coming from or picking up items that had found themselves mysteriously broken on the floor. Rarely would the couple get a full night's sleep, but if they were lucky enough to, it always seemed to bring about horrible, unsettling dreams.

"It's this Goddamn place," Bud would say to his wife. "There's something wrong here. Something is not right. We should just get out of here, sell the place, and move. Maybe we can move to Indiana where it's quiet and relaxing. We can get a place with more land and I can start working the field and growing crops like my father used to do."

Martha would laugh it off as if he were only joking. "At your age?" she would say. "You'd break a hip before you even got a single row of corn planted." There had always been playful banter between the two of them, but they each had their reservations about leaving.

Then it seemed, for whatever reason, the strange occurrences suddenly stopped. Weeks went by without any instances of bizarre happenings. Weeks soon turned into months. Bud and Martha felt a sense of relief. They didn't want to leave the home that they had lived in for almost forty years. And now it seemed they wouldn't have to worry about it anymore.

With the peculiar events having ceased, Bud felt this was the perfect opportunity for him to convince his wife to let him focus on trying to expand their little vegetable garden into something more. Yes, he was older, but he needed something like this to keep himself preoccupied. He never had much of a chance while he was working full-time. And for the previous two years, his house seemed to have some uncontrollable spirits take up residence shortly after he retired. That alone kept him too busy to even think of anything else. With those events past him, now was the time.

He had the full support of his wife when he went out to buy the tractor. It was what he wanted to do, and he felt he deserved it. He had left his home and his family after college to become a devoted husband, leaving the farming behind him to instead get a job as a delivery driver for Federal Express.

He worked hard at FedEx, driving and delivering packages for ten to twelve hours a day, with very little time for a lunch break. He knew the longer he took a break for, the longer it would take him to finish emptying his truck to end his shift. He had been a very dedicated and determined employee for nearly forty years.

With his determination, there was no doubt that he would have had a full field of vegetables to harvest had he had the opportunity to finish what he started. That, however, was not going to be the case.

While driving the tractor out into the field, just three days after having purchased it, he managed to get the front left tire stuck in a mud patch. He never noticed the area being muddy like this before, yet here he was with the front driver's side tire of his new tractor spinning freely without getting enough traction to move forward. He turned the tractor off to investigate what the problem was. There wasn't an abundance of mud by any means, and the tire wasn't very deep into it at all. It should be able to plow right through it without pause. Baffled by the tractor's inability to break free from the mire, he stood there for several minutes staring at it and scratching his head trying to devise a plan to free the large piece of equipment. Finally, he yelled to his wife who had been watching the scene play out from the kitchen window.

"Martha, can you bring me the shovel from the garage?"

With an amused look on her face, she shouted back, "Are you sure you come from a long line of farmers?" The jibes were never meant as anything more than simply having fun.

"You'll see," Bud yelled back, "we'll have crops before you know it. If you ever get out here with that shovel, that is."

Moments later, with a shovel in hand, Martha was making her way to her husband who she could see was kneeling by the front tire using his hand in a strange motion. It looked almost like he was trying to clear away something from the ground. She couldn't see anything present, but there he was, all the same, flinging his hand over his shoulder as if throwing something over it. Suddenly, without warning, the tractor lurched forward a couple of feet pinning Bud underneath its full weight. In a panic, Martha dropped the shovel and ran to her husband who was not moving at all.

"Bud, oh my God. What do I do? What do I do?"

She could see he was conscious, but his breathing was very shallow. Instinctively she pressed against the tractor to try to get it to move. The massive machinery wouldn't budge of course. The tractor wasn't turned on, and she had no idea how to even start it, let alone move it.

"I've got to get some help! You're gonna be ok. You're gonna be ok. I've got to get the phone. Just hold on Bud! I'm coming right back. Just hold on!"

As quickly as she could, Martha ran back to the house to retrieve the phone. Her heart racing, she couldn't stop her hands from shaking as she dialed 911. Everything seemed to be taking forever. She was in hysterics as she did her best to relay the information to the operator. Still clutching the phone, she ran back outside to be with her husband and to let him know that help was on the way. When she arrived back at her husband's side, she couldn't tell if he was still breathing or not. She again tried pushing the tractor but with no success.

"Stay with me Bud, please stay with me! Don't do this to me!" she shouted. "No, no, please!" She slammed her fists into the tire several times in frustration and rage, hoping each time it would miraculously move. It didn't.

By the time the ambulance arrived, Martha had already known that it was too late. Her husband was gone. She was sitting by his side, leaning against the very tire that had crushed him, calmly rubbing her fingers along his face. She was in shock, and it was a struggle for the EMT's to remove her away so that they could check the body for any sign of life. She was clenching Bud's shirt in a vice-like grip, her hand shaking and turning white from the pressure. When they finally managed to pull her free, she was mumbling incoherently and she could hardly stand on her own. One of the EMT's sat her down several yards away while the other attended to her husband. After several minutes of staring blankly at the scene unfolding in front of her, Martha finally seemed rational enough to talk.

The EMT questioned her about where the key was so that they could move the tractor off of her husband's lifeless body. She had no idea where the key was, or if there was even a spare. The tractor wasn't on when she first ran to his aid.

The EMT's searched the area surrounding the tractor but could not locate any keys at all. They had no choice but to wait for other authorities to arrive that would be better equipped to remove the tractor.

Eventually, after what seemed like hours, Bud's body was free. His legs and chest were crushed. A police officer took down Martha's statement as she watched her husband's limp body being lifted onto a stretcher. Another police officer standing by the stretcher noticed two keys fall from the man's front pocket onto the ground. On a hunch, he grabbed the keys and climbed aboard the tractor. Sure enough, both keys were able to start it. They had been in the victim's pocket the entire time while he was pinned under its wheel. This was a puzzling thing since there could be no explanation as to how the tractor ended up on top of the man if he, alone, had the keys in his possession the entire time. The engine was off with no key to start it, and his pockets were not accessible the way the tractor was situated on his body.

"Ma'am," one of the officers questioned, "do you know what your husband was doing when the tractor... when the incident happened?"

Martha sat silent for a few moments; her fingers fidgeting with a tissue that was partially crumpled up in her hand.

"It... it looked like he was trying to clear away something from under the tire; like he was scooping up mud or something and tossing it away."

The officers looked around the tires of the tractor. There was no mud present at all. The ground couldn't be more solid. Whatever he was doing, they thought, it wasn't clearing away any mud. This would be written up as a freak accident; nothing more.

Martha couldn't accept that. She was there. She saw what had happened. The tractor seemed to suddenly come to life and accelerate forward. It wasn't a "freak accident" as the officer would have her believe. She knew what it was. Bud's warnings started ringing in her ears.

"It's this Goddamn place. There's something wrong here."

And that "something" was back. She thought it was gone. They both did. But she witnessed the tractor move by itself, and now her husband is dead. There was no other explanation. Whatever had been here before; turning on lights and closing doors; had returned. And it had taken from her the most important thing in her life.

Why didn't she listen to him? He wanted to leave; to get away from this place. There was something evil here. She knew that now. And although it was too late for her poor Bud, there was nothing left for her there anymore. So she did what they should have done years before. She packed up only some personal belongings and disappeared, leaving everything else behind.

The house lay dormant and cold for years. Everyone in the neighborhood had heard the story. They all knew what had happened. Eventually, the city condemned the property, and the bank took possession of it. They tried to sell it many times with no luck. Nobody wanted to buy that house after what had happened there.

Until one day…

…somebody did.

JEFF VANOUDENHOVE works as a Project Engineer for a protective packaging company. He is a fourth-degree black belt and teacher of Chung Do Kwan Tae Kwon Do which he has been training in since 1983. When he was younger, he dreamed of being a comic book writer, but later decided to tackle writing a literary book instead. *Dark Place* is the first novel he has written towards fulfilling a life-long dream.

Made in the USA
Middletown, DE
28 February 2023

25572625R00172